D1151413

LLYFRGELL CEREDIGION LIBRARY

3802196307449

SPECIAL MESSAGE TO READERS

THE ULVERSCROFT FOUNDATION
(registered UK charity number 264873)

was established in 1972 to provide funds for research, diagnosis and treatment of eye diseases. Examples of major projects funded by the Ulverscroft Foundation are:-

- The Children's Eye Unit at Moorfields Eye Hospital, London
- The Ulverscroft Children's Eye Unit at Great Ormond Street Hospital for Sick Children
- Funding research into eye diseases and treatment at the Department of Ophthalmology, University of Leicester
- The Ulverscroft Vision Research Group, Institute of Child Health
- Twin operating theatres at the Western Ophthalmic Hospital, London
- The Chair of Ophthalmology at the Royal Australian College of Ophthalmologists

You can help further the work of the Foundation by making a donation or leaving a legacy. Every contribution is gratefully received. If you would like to help support the Foundation or require further information, please contact:

THE ULVERSCROFT FOUNDATION
The Green, Bradgate Road, Anstey
Leicester LE7 7FU, England
Tel: (0116) 236 4325

website: www.foundation.ulverscroft.com

Llyfrgell Ceredigion
Ceredigion Library

THREE TRAILS

Joe Striker and Will Fawcett constantly face danger and trouble. Evading gunfights and corruption they cross the border into Arizona, where they are joined by Emer Sparrow. However, there can be no safe haven whilst each has a price on their head. So they turn south to Mexico and go separate ways to frustrate the bounty hunters and Arizona Rangers. But Ralph Finn, Muletown's crooked sheriff, has a score to settle. When the chase ends, it's not only their lives that are at stake.

Books by Abe Dancer
in the Linford Western Library:

DEATH SONG
HOG-TIED
BREVET RIDGE
RIO BONITO
TRAILING WING

Dyfed

Cl	Ac
F	963074493
S	Im

Llyfrgell   Library

ABE DANCER

THREE TRAILS

Complete and Unabridged

LINFORD
Leicester

First published in Great Britain in 2011
Robert Hale Limited
London

First Linford Edition
published 2013
by arrangement with
Robert Hale Limited
London

Copyright © 2011 by Abe Dancer
All rights reserved

British Library CIP Data

Dancer, Abe.
    Three trails. - -
    (Linford western library)
    1. Western stories.
    2. Large type books.
    I. Title II. Series
    823.9′2–dc23

    ISBN 978–1–4448–1417–0

Published by
F. A. Thorpe (Publishing)
Anstey, Leicestershire

Set by Words & Graphics Ltd.
Anstey, Leicestershire
Printed and bound in Great Britain by
T. J. International Ltd., Padstow, Cornwall

This book is printed on acid-free paper

1

The hoofs of the lone horse marked the sandy border of the creek, then they climbed the rising bankside before swinging east towards the timberline of the Sierra Nevadas.

The two riders who had been following the trail for more than a week knew they had their man now. Yule Kater, the elder of the two brothers pulled off his sweat-stained hat for a moment, scratched his straggly black hair.

'Sumbitch won't get far now, Marl,' he said. 'That timber'll slow him down. By first dark, he'll be our dead meat.'

Marlow Kater wiped the heel of his hand across his flattened nose and spat. He didn't answer Yule, but kicked his weary mount forward, urged it away from the creek.

Yule rode after his brother and when

1

he'd drawn level gave him an anxious glance. Marlow had been close to their father who'd been gunned down in an argument by the man they were chasing. To the Katers' way of thinking, it had been a fair fight, but the old man was drunk and mean as a grizzly, and had goaded the hapless ranny into reaching for his Colt. None of that amounted to a hill of beans as far as Yule and Marlow were concerned. Their father was dead, and the man who'd killed him had to suffer the punishment.

'So, if he is headed into them hills, we don't have to go bustin' a gut,' Yule continued. 'It's thick timber. By the time he finds a way through, we'll be breathin' down the back of his neck.'

'That's only if he tries to ride on through,' Marlow responded.

'Where the hell else is he goin'?'

'He can skirt around. If he does, we'll likely miss him.'

'Goin' that way will take him a couple more days.'

'Yeah, but he'd be out in the open . . . better able to watch his backtrail. He's no pilgrim,' Yule said. 'If he was, we wouldn't have been ridin' our asses off night an' day tryin' to run him to ground.'

'He don't know we're followin'.'

'Bah, he sure knows *someone* is. Why else would he cover his trail?'

'Naturally cautious. He's reason to be.'

Not thinking much of Yule's suggestion, Marlow sniffed vulgarly and spat again. Then he put spurs to his horse's dusty flanks and broke into a trot.

With no option but to follow on, Yule cursed. He puffed his grimy cheeks, shook his head miserably. 'Goddamn, sprout. What the hell do you know?' he murmured in edgy acknowledgment of Marlow being five years his junior.

★   ★   ★

Far ahead, riding under a low dirt cloud that rose from the hoofs of his

3

weary mount, the man the Katers sought headed into the foothills. He was making sure his trail could be clearly seen, but then he skirted off to the east. Using stony ground he rode hard, took time to cover his tracks when and where he could.

His name was Joe Striker. He was heavily built and his weather-beaten appearance made him look much older than he actually was. Not so long ago, a girl in San Angelo told him he'd got the face of someone who'd been to the edge of the world and looked over. He'd laughed, said he'd once spent a night in Carson City.

The horse he rode wasn't his, leastwise it hadn't been ten days previous. Then, it had belonged to the old rooster who'd provoked him into going for his gun in the main street of the Nevada border town. The man hadn't been too slow when it came to dragging an iron from his pants belt, but fortunately he'd been no match for Striker. The trouble was, a stray bullet had caught Striker's mount that had been tethered at the hitchrail.

He was warned immediately that the old man's two sons were certain to come after him and, figuring his wounded mount wouldn't carry him far, he'd ridden south on the dead man's cow pony. He knew he'd be stamped a horse-thief, but considering some of the places he'd been recently, that was almost a term of endearment.

Striker hadn't taken any chances and covered his tracks from a few miles out of town. But on the third day, he'd spotted the two riders who were pursuing him. He could have set up an ambush and nailed them there and then, but he wasn't a natural blood spiller, and there was a lot of open country if he'd missed. So, he'd pressed on, taking a little more care to cover his trail. For a time it seemed he'd managed to throw them off. But now, skirting the land that rose up to the timberline, he saw the rise of disturbed blue quail from the scrub behind him, and he wasn't so sure.

He had aimed to go over the range, follow the course of a creek through the cracked walls of the Sierras. But once he'd seen the steep bouldered slopes and wind-gnarled timber, he'd decided he'd have to take the longer route by taking the cow pony around them. By keeping to the edge of the foothills, he would at least make it, stand a better chance of coming across a town. And he needed supplies badly, for when he'd ridden out after the shooting, he had nothing more than his guns and a canteen of musty water that was hanging from the saddle horn.

He pulled his carbine from its scabbard and jacked a shell into the breech. After a quick glance at his back-trail, he slid the gun back into leather. It was a wise precaution, could save a couple of seconds when the shooting started. The men who had been following for eight days weren't about to go home now. He urged the cow pony on, hoped to make it to some sort of shelter before his pursuers caught up with him.

★   ★   ★

Two hundred miles further south, in the unforgiving cow town of Bad Bear, there was trouble looming for a man called Will Fawcett. He had come in with a trail herd of Mexican border Longhorns, collected his pay and was preparing to hit one of the town's dog-hole saloons. He purchased a bottle of mescal and he took it with him while he had a haircut, a shave and a bath. Then, after the obligatory tryst with a crib girl, he bellied up to the bar beside some of the other trail hands. But Will Fawcett was mostly a man who kept to himself, had been all the way up from Ensenada. So it wasn't long before he took what was left of his bottle and ambled across to the gambling bay.

He lost a few dollars at blackjack and faro then found a low-stakes poker game. It was run by the house, entertained a few locals and one man he'd known briefly on the trail drive. When this man folded early the house man suggested raising the stakes and everyone appeared to agree. Will went along with it, but after a few hands, he began to lose steadily, figured if it continued it wouldn't be too long before his pockets were empty. But he didn't think he was in a position to quit, and; unwisely, tried to retrieve his losses. He was considering pulling out while he still had five dollars left, when the house man won a hand with a spade flush. The only thing was, Will was certain he'd just discarded the jack of spades himself, and here it was being fanned across the table as part of the house man's hand.

Will was in his mid-thirties, tall and fair-haired. With his freshly shaven jowls and neatly combed hair he looked younger and more like a harmless tenderfoot. But if someone had looked a little longer or deeper into his grey eyes, they'd have seen a colder set, signs of forewarning. The gambler either didn't see it, or was too dumb to take note.

In one fast movement, Will's left hand seized the gambler's wrist. The man was grinning smugly as he started to rake in his winnings, but his expression froze as the trail driver's fingers gripped him.

'Hey, what's wrong feller?' he asked turning his eyes towards Will. 'My flush wins, I think.'

'Yeah, with a discarded jack,' Will said coldly. 'It was in my hand a moment or two ago.'

The tension at the table was immediately gripping. Two players scraped their chairs back across the dank sawdusted floorboards, but didn't stand. They were just making sure they could swing their feet clear of the table if they had to.

'You ain't been in town long enough to say that kind o' thing, feller,' the gambler countered, as Will released his grip. 'We don't know whether you're serious or not.'

Will didn't say anything in reply. Instead he quickly slapped the man twice across the face. 'I'm serious,' he rasped quietly. 'Leave the pot where it is.'

The gambler recoiled and took an unsteady step backwards. The other card players pushed away from the table. Some customers, seeing what was coming, scrambled for any cover they could find, in their panicky haste, even using each other.

The gambler shook his head, blinked to recover as he watched Will get to his feet, and step away from the table. Will's hand drifted assertively to the butt of his Navy Colt.

There could be only one reply to such a threat and the gambler blanched because he couldn't think of a way to back down. 'You ain't gettin' out o' here without backin' that up. I ain't no goddamn tinhorn,' he offered.

There was a slight movement of

Will's head, then a shrug as he pictured the next move. 'Ordinarily, I'd have let it ride, taken it back in a few hands,' he said. 'But right now I'm havin' a run o' bad luck, so to speak . . . can't afford to let you trick me out of a few cents even.' Being cheated had put fire into Will's belly, sparked his anger.

The gambler's right hand streaked across his body in a cross-draw for a belly Colt. The short barrel was just clearing the holster when Will's own Colt crashed out and a .36 bullet slammed low into the gambler's chest. The man staggered back, stayed on his feet until a second bullet took him a little higher.

As he crumpled to the floor, one man pushed his way through the nervy onlookers. It was the town's sheriff who had been playing poker in his customary far corner of the saloon. He was closely followed by his deputy who was already clicking back the hammer of a single-barrelled shotgun.

Will cursed and dived for the floor as

the gun thundered, and a fat ounce of buckshot ripped into the bar front. Will was rolling towards the lawmen and by the time the deputy had reloaded he was on his belly, elbows propping him steadily against the floor.

'You was here all along, goddamnit. You must've seen it was self-defence,' he shouted.

'Nope,' the deputy said, dropping the barrel down at Will.

The Colt in Will's fist kicked, and the deputy spun around, slammed a dropping shoulder against the sheriff as he went down. The shotgun sent its charge into the ceiling, bringing half a cartwheel candelabra crashing down amidst a great billow of dust. Will cursed again, leapt up and dived for the side door as the sheriff snapped a shot at him. He fired a shot back, scattering a group of men who looked like rabbits scuttling for the same exit.

The sheriff took a bemused look down at his stricken deputy then yelled out threats of hellfire and damnation.

Enraged, he fired off another shot just as a panic-struck customer ran across his line of fire. The man grunted, tripped and ran straight to the ground. He rolled on to his back, stared with surprise and disbelief as the pain exploded in his chest and blood spread quickly across the front of his shirt.

Will ignored the sheriff's raucous threats — he wasn't going to take a chance with another trigger-happy, crazy lawman — and used the chaotic moment to slip out through the door. Once outside, he ran down the alley beyond, leapt over a pile of crates and veered out on to Main. The sheriff came charging back out through the batwings. He was still yelling and shooting, and Will knew he had to stop him or die. He turned on his heel, took a short, thoughtful breath and calmly triggered off his last two shots. The stricken sheriff hardly moved. He attempted a cruel smile, then, as if someone had hacked away his legs he fell heavily, his big .44 Colt dropping from his lifeless fingers on to the boardwalk.

Will kept running towards the livery. He cleared town less than ten minutes later, racing his sorrel towards the protective maw of darkness.

2

Joe Striker didn't even know the name of the town until he went into the mercantile and telegraph office. He saw the words, Slater Wells in faded yellow paint on the window above the operator's cubicle.

His provisions almost cleaned him out; the couple of dollars he had left was enough to buy him a few drinks and a meal. But lack of money wasn't his only problem. Joe was fully aware that two relentless pursuers were still somewhere along his backtrail.

Late yesterday he'd seen them in the distance when he'd swung towards the mountains. They were silhouetted where the sun dropped into the San Joaquin Valley, and Joe had instantly grinned at what he considered foolhardy. But the riders soon dropped from sight when they rode into a long,

15

shallow depression. Although it would have been a lot easier to avoid it, he'd ridden through there himself, and deliberately. The fact that the two riders had followed on, showed that they were sticking to his trail, or as much of it as they could pick up. 'Stringin' me a couple o' greeners,' he'd muttered aloud.

Joe had ridden for a long time that night, managing to increase the distance between him and his pursuers. He'd taken time to lay out a pattern of confusing tracks, make it seem as if he'd veered away from the town. If they were who he thought they were, they'd know he was still riding their pa's cow pony, would figure he'd try and avoid a confrontation with the law in Slater Wells. So, he'd doubled back at daybreak and entered the town just before mid-morning.

Now, Joe could decide whether to ride on through, or take time out for a couple of drinks and some decent fixings. With most of his body demanding sustenance, Joe decided to take a chance. After that, he'd clear the state line. California hadn't brought much good luck for him, so he decided to head for Arizona. It would take a week or two, but he could find work, maybe pocket some dollars as he moved along.

He drank two whiskeys and a beer in the saloon before crossing the street to a beanery.

'I'm doin' me a new line in fried chicken an' beans,' the eating-house man told him.

Joe thought for a moment then nodded. 'Sounds good. What makes it new?'

'My wife cooks it, so it's chicken. It comes with taters an' biscuits,' the man replied without taking his eyes off Joe.

'As long as she don't take all day with it. I'm thinkin' on bein' somewhere else,' Joe said. 'An' I'll have some hot jamoka,' he added with a tight smile.

For the next half-hour, he enjoyed his meal and coffee, had just enough money left to pay for it.

Unfortunately, and not long after

that, the Kater brothers made it into town. They saw Joe tying his grub-sack to the saddle cantle on their father's mount. Without warning, Marlow swung his rifle up, but such was the general quietness of the town at that hour, that the unmistakable sound of the lever action carried along the street. Joe turned, his right hand already darting for his Colt.

The rifle and six-gun crashed out together, but it was Marlow who was hit. The man threw up his arms, collapsed sideways from his rearing mount. The rifle's bullet chewed out a splinter from the hitch rail beside Joe, and the cow pony snorted, tearing at the reins.

By then, Yule was bellowing with rage. He cruelly spurred forward as his brother lay kicking and rolling in the dust. His gun roared and two bullets whistled close to Joe. Grimly taking a bead on the charging rider, Joe drew back the hammer of his Colt and fired once. Yule Kater slammed back over the rump of his galloping mount and crashed to the ground. He rolled into the dirt of the street and attempted to make a last spit with his face down turned.

Joe caught a movement out of the corner of his eye and turned to see Marlow was getting to his knees. Joe looked distastefully at the rill of bright blood that trickled from the corner of his mouth, and he fired once again. The bullet plugged into the dirt between the man's legs, stopped him from dying.

'Should've stuck to the chase,' he rasped. 'It's safer than the kill.'

From further down the street a door crashed open. Joe brought his Colt up, watched uneasily as the evening sun blazed briefly on a lawman's star. A tall man with a thick black beard and carrying a prod pole, stepped into the street and started walking towards him.

Joe held the Colt down at his side, but coolly drew back the hammer.

'Put the hogleg away,' the sheriff ordered.

19

Joe didn't move, his expression uncertain, but vigilant.

The sheriff looked irritated, but he didn't push for anything more. 'I seen most o' what just happened. Saw it from the roof window above my jail,' he explained. 'Looked to me like them fellers came gunnin' for you. You care to tell an old badgeman why?'

'It was more'n a week ago . . . a few miles north o' here,' Joe started. 'Their ol' man got himself liquored up an' was spoilin' for a fight. I had to protect myself, an' he died 'cause of it.'

'You *had to*, eh?' the sheriff echoed. 'Huh, if I had a dollar for every time I heard that, I'd want for nothin' in this world.'

'It was the only way out, Sheriff. Just like them two. Some folk never learn.'

'Maybe not,' the sheriff replied brusquely. 'But it's a rare kind o' man that shoots another in cold blood. That's why I carry this ol' sticker.'

Joe was about to respond with a few

cutting words when one of the towns-folk who'd gathered at the sound of the shooting, called out from the board-walk.

'Hey, Sheriff, they're the Kater brothers. Dead one's Yule. I seen 'em in the Fresno stockyards a few times.'

'It was Ike Kater, their pa you killed?' the sheriff said turning back to Joe.

Joe shook his head ingenuously. 'We never got to swappin' names.'

The lawman nodded slowly and thoughtfully. 'From what I heard, them's real mean sons o' bitches . . . real sinners. But what you done ain't exactly God's work, so I'm askin' you to move on.'

Joe suddenly looked a tad mulish. He had no reason to stay, but he wanted it to be his decision, not someone else's.

'All of a sudden, sheets on a bed an' head on a pillow, feels real welcomin'. Maybe I'll stay the night,' he suggested wryly.

The lawman shook his head. 'There's been enough mistakes made here for

21

one day, son. You don't want to be another one,' he warned. 'Move on. An' don't stop at any county line,' he added suddenly. 'If the brand on that mount you're ridin' is what I think it is, things could get kind o' sticky for you in this neck o' the woods.'

Joe didn't like the provocation or the threat. But he swung up into the saddle and, without looking back, rode off. On the outskirts of town, he raised a hand in farewell to an old man who was driving an empty calf wagon. 'Good luck,' he called out.

3

After quitting Bad Bear, Will Fawcett headed north, then east. He was only two or three days' ride from the Arizona state line, and he'd heard there were plenty of opportunities for a man who could work cattle.

He crossed the Colorado River to find work on a spread three miles outside the town of Growler. Everything went well for a couple of weeks, then came payday and a Saturday night in town.

He was standing at the bar having a few drinks, idly playing chuck-a-luck with the cowhands, when a soberly dressed, middle-aged man toting a sheriff's star, walked up to them. Will saw the lawman's reflection in the back-bar mirror, paused with his shot glass halfway to his mouth and cursed.

'Are you Will Fawcett?' the man

asked in an affable enough manner.

Will turned slowly and nodded. 'Yeah, I'm him. What's he done now?' he asked with a weary smile.

'Someone here says they recognize you from a public notice dodger. Now I'm here, it sure looks like you could be him. Does Bad Bear mean anythin' to you?'

'It's a town I've been to,' Will said warily.

'Recent?'

Will shrugged. The other cowboys eyed him keenly as the memory of Bad Bear's gun-crazed lawmen flashed through his mind.

'This Fawcett killed two men. A saloon gambler an' a sheriff, no less. He also put a bullet in a deputy,' the sheriff said.

'Surely a mistake, Sheriff,' Will suggested ambiguously.

'Well, that's how we learn. An' as soon as it's put right, the sooner you can get back here to your funnin',' the sheriff told him. 'Meantime, hand over that Navy Six you're carryin'.'

Will shook his head. 'Hand over my gun, just because someone says they've seen someone who looks like someone else? That ain't real likely,' he said flatly.

'I was tellin' you, son, not askin'.' The sheriff stepped back and jerked his head up and to the right, but made no move towards his holstered Colt.

Will turned to look up towards where the sheriff had indicated. He saw two men covering him from the upstairs landing. Light from the saloon's hanging lamps glinted dully on their badges and rifles.

'Time for second thoughts?'

Will raised his shoulders indifferently. 'Hell, Sheriff, that gambler was a tinhorn. I caught him red-handed tryin' to cheat me. I was packin' my gun when that deputy came in like billy hell an' just let go. If I hadn't dived for cover, his buckshot would have plastered me across the goddamn ceilin'. It was him or me, then the actual sheriff started hurlin' lead around the place.

25

For some reason, neither of 'em wanted me to get out o' there alive.'

The lawman sniffed. 'Looks like none of us will have to bother any more about Bad Bear's sheriff an' his approach to law keepin'. But there's still a dodger out, son, an' it's still my duty to take you in. So don't go attemptin' anythin' stupid. I ain't always this considerate.'

Will glanced again at the two deputies. Then, he lifted his Colt, at the sheriffs caution, used only finger and thumb on the butt. As he handed it over, he pretended to lose his grip. The gun dropped, and the sheriff instinctively stepped forward to make a grab as it fell.

But Will was already moving with the speed and agility of a falling cat. He went down on one knee, caught the gun as it hit the floor, then with one long rising movement, got up tight behind the sheriff. He locked his left arm around the man's neck and pressed the long barrel of his Colt hard against the base of the man's spine.

'I really ain't a sheriff killer,' he rasped out to the riflemen. 'An' if you don't lower them rifles, this one'll be spendin' the rest of his life in a wheelchair.'

The deputies hesitated for a moment, then complied. The sheriff made a sudden grab for his own Colt, but Will cracked his wrist. 'With one arm,' he added harshly.

'Now raise your hands,' he said and punched a shot close above the heads of the deputies. One of them dropped his rifle at his feet, and thrust his hands out, palms facing down. The other man took advantage of Will's brief distraction, lifted his rifle and fired hurriedly. But he wasn't a sheriff killer either.

Will cursed and dropped to one knee. He pushed the sheriff sideways, as the rifle bullet plugged into the floor a yard from his feet.

Above him, the deputy stood there gaping in shock at what he'd almost accomplished. Will calmly shot him in the arm and the smoking rifle flew from his grip. It fell to the saloon below, crashed on to a table that scattered glasses, bottles, cards and players alike. The other man still held his hands out, shaking his head with non-involvement.

Will looked at the sheriff, gave a half-smile, half-grimace. He straightened and, looking at the men he'd recently been riding the range with, started backing towards the batwings. 'I guess the sheriff'll say what happened here,' he said. 'I hope some of you'll make sure it's right.'

The sheriff gave a grateful nod in acknowledgment of maybe having his life saved, and Will pushed his way from the saloon. Out on the boardwalk, he loosed off a frustrated air shot, rammed his Colt back into his holster and swung doggedly into the saddle.

Less than a minute later, he cleared town and swung east. 'I'll try gettin' drowned in that big Gila Lake,' he threatened with weary, dark humour.

4

Mindful of a debt, the sheriff of Slater Wells had only given Joe Striker a head start. In due course, he had issued a wanted poster that included a hundred-dollar reward for Joe's capture.

Joe picked up the chase early on and for nearly two days rode well ahead. Stirred by the reward money, the makeshift posse was speculative and wary, they didn't really want a close encounter with Joe's guns.

Broke and hungry, and still a long ride from the Arizona border, it was a sense other than sight or sound that told Joe something was wrong. He was returning to his small camp with extra brushwood to build up his night fire. He stopped and looked around him, drew his Colt and buried it in the armful of firewood before walking in.

The stranger, hunkered by the

smouldering fire, was staring pensively into Joe's coffee can. He wore a long, stained dustcoat and a greasy derby above his dark, stubbled face. When he looked up and grinned a mouthful of broken teeth, Joe's instant thought was, out-of-state ranger.

The man set down the mug and slowly stood up. 'Hope you don't mind, feller,' he said. 'Smelled it from a ways off. I'm down to crushin' beetles underfoot. Run out o' grub too. Figured we might do a trade. Name's Brinner.'

Joe stared at him coldly, noted that the man's grey mare showed signs of being ridden hard. The spur marks on its flanks were raw and blood flecked. 'Yeah, well, one o' you's sure got lathered up,' he replied. 'You must be real desperate. My coffee don't normally draw such interest.'

'I gave a shout,' the man said. 'But this ain't the sort o' territory you like to give too much away.'

'Ain't that the truth,' Joe agreed, his

eyes scouring the gloom for any other sign of movement. 'Just as well you didn't bring any friends along.'

'I'm alone, Striker. Like I said, it was . . . '

The man realized straight off he'd blundered by mentioning Joe's name. He groaned his frustration and kicked the coffee mug. At the same time he swept back his coat to reveal a shotgun that had been sawn off at both the stock and the barrel. It was attached to a rawhide thong that hung from his belt, and he snapped it up in the bat of an eye.

But Joe had the advantage, held the edge ever since he'd approached his camp-fire. The stack of wood dropped away from his hands and his Colt blazed out. His bullet hit the man in the chest, punching him fast backwards. As the man died, he fell towards the fire and his shotgun thundered a single blast across the darkness.

'You're a goddamn bounty hunter,' Joe seethed. His left leg felt like it had been bitten by a dog and stung bad as it started to fold beneath him. But he heard a noise behind him and twisted around. As he fell, he saw the shadow of a second man riding from left to right in the murk. Joe fired, squirmed painfully on to his belly, raised his Colt and fired again.

But the rider was gone. He kept going, crashed his mount through the scrub, making no attempt to return fire. Joe sent a final shot after him, then lurched to his feet. In the low light he saw that his left leg was bleeding profusely. He swore and limped across to where he'd tethered his horse. It was standing as if rooted to the spot, wide-eyed and fearful. The dead man's mount that had run off, now came back, slowly pawing the ground at each wary step.

Joe swung into his saddle and, quickly figuring he might need a change of horse, caught the reins of the grey mare as he rode by. If those two goddamn bounty men could locate him, then so could a posse. And it was still a long ride to the state line.

Switching from horse to horse, hardly pausing for rest, he rode for many long hours. It was obvious he was making for Arizona, so there wasn't much point in covering his trail. In the early morning, he rode along a narrow creek that was edged with sedge and strewn with moss-covered boulders. His leg was now badly swollen, and he decided to take the time to dig out the buckshot. If he didn't do something, he was afraid a bad sort of sepsis would set in.

It was a raw and painful job prising out the pellets, and with no spirit to clean or cauterize, he stuffed the puncture wounds with tufts of damp moss. He bandaged his leg with the arm of his spare shirt, then limped to his horse and swung back into the saddle. It wasn't long before he felt weak and sick. He wanted to rest up and sleep, but he'd already lost much time in tending his wounds. He had to ride fast, and so trusted the sharp, soreness from his leg to keep him awake and concentrated.

He made it to a break in the Chocolate Mountains and surveyed the wild land that stretched away on all sides with little or no cover. But he had no choice; he had to make a run for the Arizona border and a ring of low mountain ranges.

After another six hours of painful riding he glanced back and his heart sank. A small group of riders was approaching across the scrubby flats. They were riding at a good clip and were unquestionably closing in on him.

Joe still had a good lead, but both his mounts were weary now and he knew he would be lucky to reach the border before the posse caught up with him. He checked his Colt and rifle, spurred his mount into a canter. Then he saw a low-walled drywash and rode down into it, making better time along the flatter, more even ground.

But even as he cleared the eastern end, the first of the chasing riders came within range and he heard the dull crack of rifles behind him. By the time he reached the Gila River, he was cursing aloud with bullets whistling all around him. He plunged his mount into the rushing water and hauled out his rifle. Hipping around in the saddle he levered and triggered as fast as he could, forcing the possemen to stay back and search for cover. When his rifle was empty he sheathed it and drew his Colt, but the possemen were out of range.

'*Adios, amigos,*' he shouted excitedly, kicked with his good leg as the cow pony heaved and bucked beneath him. Minutes later they struggled up the far bank, on and up to a high table and deeper into Arizona. Joe guessed that whatever the bounty on him was, it wasn't worth the posse making the crossing, and he was right. They stayed on the California side, but sent a hail of bullets after him as he rode further east. No doubt the failed riders would wire on ahead to say Joe Striker was now in Arizona; the invitation for a backshooter to gain some reward money.

5

Will Fawcett cursed silently as he watched from the ridge while the ramrod detailed five men for nighthawk duty. In a deep blaze of colour, the sun was setting behind the hills that encircled the roundup camp in the gorge below him.

He'd picked the wrong herd to rustle, and in frustration, he rested his head on his forearms. There were just too many riders night-herding. But the way his luck had been running lately, it was nothing more than he expected. With the trouble that had followed him from Bad Bear and then Growler, he'd been forced into lawless ways. Avoiding posses and small town lawmen had kept him dodging all over the territory east and west of the Colorado River.

Will knew many an owlhoot rider who claimed the same thing. Apart from one or two notable exceptions, almost every outlaw he'd ever met swore he was innocent of the crimes he'd been accused of or charged with. Will had usually smiled indulgently at their resentfullness, but now he was willing to concede that some of them were maybe telling the truth.

The trouble *he* was in, hadn't been of his own making. The four-flush gambler and the trigger-happy lawmen were the ones at fault. But Will wasn't going to spend time dishing out futile blame. He had places to go and a lot of things yet to do. Without running the risk of someone recognizing him and calling in the law, he'd figured the best thing would be to work for himself, start his own cattle business. He could handle a gun and rope and ride well and he knew cattle. He also had the uncertain gain of being literate.

Will's mother and father had been a contract trail driver and cook, and consequently he'd grown up in the saddle. But when he was ten, his mother was killed when her coaster was struck by lightning on a Colorado River crossing. Will was instantly a burden for his father and he'd been boarded with friends or placed in an orphanage. It was during those long spells that he'd attended school, learned to read and write.

A few years later, when he was fifteen, his father's own herd had been stricken by Spanish fever and everything he might have inherited disappeared in a pyre of incineration smoke. A broken man, his father disappeared, and Will was left with the clothes he stood up in, a rifle, a Navy Colt and a switch-tail mare.

Will was soon to learn that, if he wanted to survive he had to be able to fight. Right now seemed like an opportune time to make use of the skills he'd acquired over the years, and he went into the business of rustling.

Other than the threat of a renegade Texas ranger, the canyon country was an ideal place to practise such a calling.

Once a man rode away from the bigger towns that were strung out along the state line, the law wasn't all that common. As long as you didn't go too far east towards the Eagle Tail Mountains, the land was reasonably fertile, could support medium-sized herds. There were huge tracts of free land, and isolated slick-rock gorges could be used for holding steers while brands were blotched. For herds driven up from Mexico, it was excellent outlaw country.

The first herd he'd hit, had been down on the Feraz Mesa. The steers had grown used to being left to their own devices, and with bellies so full of grass, he'd had little trouble in moving them north across the Gila river. It took one day to drive the herd into higher country to his secluded canyon, another day of gruelling work on the brands, then another day's drive to a sundown ranch on the outskirts of Dome Rocks. The transaction made him the fitting sum of one hundred dollars.

The second time he hadn't been quite so lucky. He found a bunch of mavericks that had been rounded up and coralled while the range riders scouted for more. No one was in the camp, so he'd moved in and helped himself to the prime, unbranded calves. But without the steadying influence of cows, he'd had the devil's own job of keeping the youngsters in a gather. Eventually, the cowboys were hot on his trail and he'd had to abandon the whole herd, make a run for it into the Eagle Tails.

That had been little more than a week ago, and now he'd picked a losing hand again. A herd with five or six nighthawks posted was no herd for Will to tackle. So he backed off the ridge and rode thoughtfully west in the direction of his hideout. He was riding along the north bank of the Gila, was deep in thought when he came across the site of a ranch nestled in a broad bend of the river. There was a small house cloaked in darkness, didn't appear to be anything to stop him running off a good-sized cut of the herd.

He sat for a while to get his bearings from the stars, until he worked out a getaway deal. If he drove the cattle from its rough pasture and cut back through a fold in the hills, he would enter canyon country sometime after first light. Provided the beeves didn't give him any trouble, he would be back in his hideout by noon.

★   ★   ★

As Will circled the herd in the pasture furthest from the ranch house, he offered a few half-hearted notes of 'Git Along, Little Dogies' to put the animals at their ease. He'd already lowered the fence rails and had started to haze the cows up that way. After riding through a cedar brake, he paused for a moment to get a rough idea of how many steers he was moving. He was about to walk off, when the muzzle of a gun was suddenly pressed hard against the nape of his neck.

'I been watchin' you for a spell, feller. Just what in hell do you think you're up to?' Joe Striker demanded.

Will flinched, then cursed. 'What the hell does it look like I'm up to?' he responded instinctively, searching for a moment's thought. 'I drew the short straw for nighthawk duty.'

Joe gave a short, grating laugh. 'Hogwash. I've been watchin' you softfootin' around for more'n an hour. Since when do nighthawks start drivin' beeves from their home pasture in the middle o' the night?'

'Boss's orders,' Will said offhand. 'Got to move 'em to another pasture. So who the hell's wantin' to know?'

Joe gave a tolerant chuckle. 'The man who'd already decided to move 'em to another pasture,' he then snapped back. 'So, are you goin' to die where you sit, or are you ridin' on? Sorry, but them's your choices.'

'Very generous,' Will agreed. 'I'll take

the ridin' option.' He turned his head against the pressure of the rifle muzzle, but it pressed deeper into his flesh. 'It's a lot o' beef for one rider to reasonably handle,' he continued. 'So if you're interested, how about we help each other?'

'Huh, help's usually a loaded proposal,' Joe sneered. 'An' partners is a state of affairs I don't usually rub along with.'

'Well that's somethin' we got in common,' Will said. 'All I'm sayin' is, if we work together, I know a place we could fill with cattle by noon tomorrow. An' I've got a market. What do you reckon?'

Joe pondered for a while, then he said. 'I reckon you must be on the dodge, or usin' a real long rope.'

'I ain't on the stump for town mayor, that's for sure,' Will answered back. 'Yeah, I'm on the dodge, but it ain't for cattle rustlin'.'

'What then?'

Will hesitated. 'A little trouble in a

44

place called Bad Ass Bear, or some place like it. Goddamn tinhorn an' a deputy sheriff got 'emselves killed.'

Joe cursed slowly, then gave a knowing smile. 'Got 'emselves killed by a turkey named Fawcett,' he said. 'Is that you?'

Will was a little surprised at Joe's lowdown. 'Yeah, Will Fawcett. How'd you get hold o' that?' he asked.

'Saw a reward notice. I like to know who the law's got in its sights. You also troubled the sheriff of Growler.'

'Judas Priest, they're sure leavin' nothin' out,' Will rasped tiresomely. 'How about you? You got a backtrail to watch?' he then wanted to know.

Joe nodded. 'Could be some bounty hunters tryin' to catch up with me . . . a posse or two, maybe,' he said quietly and just short of a wry smile.

Will shook his head with not too much surprise and turned around to face Joe. But this time Joe didn't stop him, just kept his rifle levelled.

'This jawbone's real informative,' Will

started. 'But them beeves are driftin' up close to where I lowered the rails in the fence. Be a real shame to let 'em just wander off. What do you say?'

Joe considered Will's suggestion for a moment, then lowered his rifle. 'We drive 'em to your place, change the brands an' sell 'em. Then we divvy up the take, an' go our separate ways,' he said by way of confirmation. 'An' we ain't partners,' he added hurriedly.

'More or less what I got in mind,' Will settled. 'Let's move 'em out before they walk all the way to Yuma.'

6

Black Lodge was a hotchpotch of featureless buildings set in a wasteland of low scrub and stunted trees. It was a covert rendezvous for killers and gunrunners, failed prospectors, robbers and renegades of every description, and it didn't feature on any map.

In the midst of this edgy ferment was a tall, thin Chinaman who went by the name of Whiskey John. Rumour was, he'd made money from the California gold rush, and he wore store-bought black suits and a secure smile. He handled most transactions in and around the community, and very little was bought or sold without his say so. He welcomed newcomers, although if he had the slightest suspicion one of them might be an undercover agent from Texas or California, the man was usually found sleeping toes up in the prickly pear.

The law in canyon country was thinly spread and usually not too well organized. They knew Black Lodge existed, but for many reasons hadn't been able to coordinate a break-in. And so far, Will Fawcett and Joe Striker hadn't committed any crime serious enough to bring a US marshal into Arizona Territory.

Whiskey John usually accepted the lifestyle of anyone who rode into the settlement, but it didn't entitle them to much. He might do a deal, buy whatever a man had to sell, but he rarely allowed anyone to leave with more than a dollar or two in his pocket. His henchmen saw that visitors were relieved of their cash at the crude bar in the canvas-walled saloon, at the card tables, or in the tents that housed his working girls.

'You got fine bunch o' lard, boys.' Whiskey John said as he stood on the rough boards that fronted the saloon. The cattle Joe and Will had driven in, were now in pole corrals that had been put up nearby. The Chinaman grinned, wheezed routinely after pulling a fat cigar from his lips. 'Give one dollar a head,' he said by way of an offer.

'Hah. Always heard you fellers had a real peculiar sense o' fun,' Joe replied. 'Make that five, an' we got a deal. You understand that, John?'

Whiskey John crooked an eyebrow, shook his head amusedly. 'Where you think you are, Dodge City?' he asked. 'You boys want top dollar, you better start drivin' east. I offer you goin' rate, but seein' as we both want business, I'll raise to one dollar an' a half. We got an outlaw market, in the middle of a godforsaken land where we're all heathens. So, nothin' here gets improved. Now, do you understand?'

'Your goin' rate's a long way below the five we was thinkin'. Hell, you got the outlets to get seven or eight, anyplace you want to push 'em,' Will responded, ignoring the challenging stares of the men who stood around.

'Ah, you understand it's me who's got outlets, but you forget my expenses,' the Chinaman came back quickly. 'You think I just push steers on to open market an' rake in agent's price? Hell, I got to pay to get 'em eased in. I got to pay some fellers to drive 'em out o' here an' there could be lawmen to square. No, sorry, boys, a dollar and a half's top. Come an' have a good drink on Whiskey John while you think.'

The floor of the Chinaman's big tent was hard-packed dirt and the furniture was mostly fashioned from packing cases and crates. The bar consisted of a few planks resting across some empty whiskey kegs and the bottles of rotgut were stacked in cheap crates behind it. The bartender was a huge man with small, piggy eyes that were set deep in the largest skull that Will had ever seen. He was undisputedly one of the ugliest, and the way he looked at the newcomers, it looked like he'd rather eat them than serve them drinks.

'Hog, you give these two boys a drink

on the house,' Whiskey John told the man and started to turn away. 'By the way, if you decide to hedge, there's my inconvenience penalty to consider. That means price goes back to one dollar,' he said, still smiling at Joe and Will. 'I'll be over here when you make up your minds.'

Blowing a thin curl of cigar smoke, and surrounded by four henchmen, Whiskey John went to the only genuine four-legged table in a corner of the malodorous room.

The rotgut was exactly that, and Will grimaced as he punished his throat with the raw spirit. 'You recall tellin' me about Slater Wells bein' a hell hole?' he said.

'Yeah, I was wrong,' Joe replied grimly. He had a jumpy look to him, didn't seem to notice the rawness of what they were drinking. As he sipped, he was giving Whiskey John a long, thoughtful stare.

'We might as well take his money,' Will said quietly. 'Two hundred head gives us one hundred fifty apiece.'

'It ain't enough.'

'Well we ain't in much of a position to dicker.'

'I don't like bein' bulldogged,' Joe snapped. 'Specially by a goddamn smiley, smokin' Chinaman.'

'It's *his* town. His town an' *his* law. But think on it, Joe,' Will advised. 'We didn't lose much sweat gettin' here, an' we never raised the critters. Besides, we ain't ever goin' to make our fortunes with shirt-tail rustlin'. Why don't we just accept his deal an' vamoose? We can find us an open border town . . . storm the puncheons for a day or two.'

Joe frowned then nodded. 'Yeah, you're right. I just don't like movin' on when it's someone else's idea.' Without any more discussion, Joe turned and slammed his hand flat on the bar planks. 'Hey, John, we'll take your offer,' he called across the smoke-hazed room.

The Chinaman looked up and smiled. 'It's *Mr* John,' he said, and cupped a hand to his ear.

Joe ground his jaw. He flicked a glance at Will who was staring ahead, poker-faced. 'Sure,' he answered tightly, 'I was forgettin' my manners.'

'Hah, easy in a place like this,' Whiskey John said. Then he took out a well-stuffed wallet and counted out a few bills and placed them carefully on the table. Will and Joe exchanged a fast glance because it obviously wasn't anywhere near $300. When they walked across to check, they found it to be exactly fifty.

Whiskey John smiled calmly at the puzzled looks on the outlaw's faces. 'That's on account, boys,' he said. 'You let me know when you've spent that, an' I give you another fifty. That OK? Don't worry, I can do math. I owe you two hundred an' fifty bucks after this. Now go have another drink, get yourself some girls an' have real good time.'

'Thank you, but we decided to move on,' Will said. 'So, if you give us the rest o' the money now . . . '

Whiskey John studied the end of his cigar for a moment, then glanced at Joe. 'That right? You go too?' he asked.

'Yeah. That's what the man said. I go too.'

The Chinaman's affable manner suddenly disappeared, and his black eyes chilled. 'That ain't the way things work out here, boys. I do you big favour an' buy your steers and not ask questions. In return, you spend money here in Black Lodge. We got everythin' you want . . . everythin' you like. We got liquor, girls, games. Hah, what we haven't got is the sheriff checkin' on you.' The man pointed with his cigar, indicated somewhere beyond his old campaign tent. 'There's a shack you can use for a small rent, say one dollar a night. As for everythin' else . . . help yourself,' he continued, his smile returning.

'We'll settle for the money,' Will said stubbornly. 'An' we'll decide where we're goin' to spend it.'

'Sure, I already said.' Whiskey John

jerked his head towards his henchmen. 'My boys here will show you where those places are.'

Joe immediately railed at the Chinaman's provocation. 'You owe us, you son-of-a-bitch,' he snarled, taking a menacing step forward. He snatched the notes from the table, turned for a quick few words with Will. 'Now's a real good time to become partners,' he suggested wryly.

Whiskey John's men started forward, but Will was already moving. He lifted and heaved the table into the Chinaman, then reached for his Colt, turned and fired as he dived to the floor. One of the bodyguards raised his hands, gasped and staggered backwards. He fell against the wall, tore through the badly weathered canvas and went sprawling into the ground outside. Will rolled, triggered and fired again. His second shot took another man high, and he screamed as the bullet shattered his shoulder bones.

Whiskey John was on his hands and

knees crawling rapidly for the protection of the bar. Will saw Hog raising a heavy plank above his head, preparing to hurl it towards him and Joe. He made another roll in the stinking dirt and fired upwards. Hog's body shook and he stopped, but only for a moment. Then he lumbered a couple of steps forward, with a roar of rage hurled the plank across the room. Will yelled a warning to his partner, and got to his knees. Joe stepped over one man he'd shot and cracked the barrel of his Colt across another's head before putting two bullets into Hog's huge chest.

The giant bartender stopped in his tracks. He attempted a curse as he slowly sagged to his knees, his hands clutching his bloody wounds. Will got to his feet and ran for the bar. He caught Whiskey John unslinging a shotgun from under one of the planks. The Chinaman moved very quickly, managed to swing the gun up as he thumbed back the twin hammers. Will shot him point blank and he went down, the unfired shotgun falling from his lifeless fingers.

The bout of thunderous shooting had drawn in other inhabitants of the criminal settlement. The few who were opportunist aides to Whiskey John, pushed their way into the saloon with guns drawn. While Joe was feverishly reloading, Will rammed his Colt into his holster, picked up the shotgun and fired one barrel over the heads of the advancing men. As they cursed and sought immediate cover, Will fired the second barrel at another section of the canvas wall. Then he flung the weapon aside and drew his Colt again.

'Let's go find them border towns,' he yelled to Joe as he dived through the tattered canvas. He hit the ground outside the saloon, rolled and came to his feet as Joe came hurtling after him a few seconds later. Breathless and wound up they sprinted for the corrals where their mounts were tethered. A minute later they leapt into leather, wheeled away as some of the owlhoots opened up with half-hearted gunfire.

Crouching low, they cleared the spread of ramshackle buildings at full gallop. They headed straight for open country, then turned west, back towards the foothills of the Chocolate Mountains. They didn't slow down until they reached the first low ridge where they drew rein to give their mounts a rest.

After a few moments compassing their backtrail, Joe gave Will a twisted grin. 'Where the hell did you learn to shoot like that?' he asked.

'I was goin' to ask the same o' you,' Joe replied as he drew Whiskey John's wallet from his vest. 'The Chinaman said we was to help ourselves to anythin' else we wanted,' he explained. 'With this, we got a grubstake.'

'We got a grubstake?' Will questioned. 'I thought we were goin' our own ways?'

Joe gave a slight grimace as he nodded. 'Yeah, but now I'm thinkin' we make a fair team.'

Will gave quick and serious consideration to Joe's words. 'Yeah, in a rootin', tootin' sort o' way. But I don't want to spend the rest o' my life like that, Joe. There must be a break point in escapin' before you get shot to pieces.'

'Yeah, but that was some lousy deal we were bein' presented with. Countin' these notes, we've only got even on the value o' the herd. At least, we're ridin' away, which is a lot more'n you can say for most o' them turkeys.'

The pair rode through the hills for another two days before they crossed a trail on a fork of the Bill Williams River. Twenty more miles and they came across a battered sign post that pointed north along the Big Sandy. They barely made out a few branded words on the wind-scoured wood, that said: Mule five miles. Will knew it to be a stage station and cow town that nestled in the desert mesa. Further north lay Boulder City, but Joe said the law there would probably have received the Wanted dodgers on them.

'D'you reckon there's a hundred bucks worth of entertainment in Mule?' Will asked.

'There will be after we've been there for an hour or so,' Joe said and grinned.

'Yeah, perhaps I meant distraction. Let's go an' see how it works out, Mr Fawcett,' Joe said thrusting out his hand.

'Be a pleasure, *Mr Striker*,' he agreed and returned the firm handshake.

7

Muletown was a small stage station and cow town of less than 200 souls. But the population swelled when a trail herd passed through travelling south to Yuma or north to Lake Mead. Accordingly, the sheriff needed to be tough and determined. Ralph Finn was just that. His brother Lloyd held similar qualities; among other business activities he ran the saloon. He employed a string of toughs to help keep order when the trail men were kicking up their heels, even provided his brother with deputies, if and when necessary.

Between them, the Finns more or less controlled Muletown. Lloyd owned much of the land in and around the town, and it was an open secret that Ralph was his silent partner in the property business. In return, the saloon was allowed to stay open twenty-four hours a day when a trail herd was in town.

Men who complained about crooked dealings at the card tables were frequently gun whipped and thrown into a cell. The following morning they'd be listed as drunk and disorderly and fined whatever amount of money they carried in their pockets. After paying the fines the men would be penniless, then charged with vagrancy — a civic offence which carried a mandatory thirty days in the cells — or given orders to quit town. The townsfolk themselves fared no better at the hands of the Finns. Lloyd had acquired a couple of businesses due to the fact he was also the main stockholder of the Muletown Bank. It was a position that afforded him prior knowledge of when mortgages were overdue, when property was to be sold for the arrears. In his official capacity, Ralph was always on hand to see there was no trouble when Lloyd paid the arrears and took over the business or properties. All in all,

Muletown and the Finn brothers weren't too unlike Whiskey John and his Black Lodge camp.

Lloyd was the younger, a man in his mid-twenties, amiable, well turned out and usually bathed and shaved. Every girl who worked in his saloon had been the recipient of his attention at some time or another. The sole purpose of their employ was to part customers from as much money as possible in as short a time as possible. Their way of doing it had to be within the law, and fifty per cent of all their earnings went back to the house coffers. If Lloyd desired the company of any one in particular, it was an added bonus because he was a generous client.

However, one girl called Emer Sparrow, wasn't for yielding to Lloyd's visceral attentions. One night when he entered her room uninvited, she rounded on him furiously. Her grey eyes blazed as he twisted the key in the lock of the door behind him.

'What do you think you're doin'?' she

snapped. Emer was a redhead and possessed of the renowned flaming temper. She was in her early twenties and tall. She started to grope around the small dressing table behind her for her silver-backed hair brush. 'I'm not one o' your crib girls. Get the hell out o' my room.'

Finn smoothed his narrow moustache with his forefinger. Then he shrugged out of his silver-grey coat, revealing a shoulder harness and bolstered derringer. He laid the coat across the back of a chair then made to undo his string tie.

'Take it easy, sister,' he said, retaining an unctuous smile. 'You still got an hour before you're out front. In this town it pays to have an advantage, an' this could be yours.'

Pushing his luck, the man removed his gunrig and draped it across his coat. But then he suddenly got confused as a warm smile broke across Emer's face, the way she took a hopeful step towards him.

But it was a deception for what Emer did next. She gritted her teeth and made a grab for the derringer. In one smooth movement she levelled it and cocked the hammer.

Finn's eye's widened with doubt. 'Unless I ain't understandin' what's goin' on here, you got a funny notion of how this sort o' thing's done,' he offered tentatively.

Emer shook her head, returned a chilly smile. 'I know how you do this sort o' thing,' she flung back. 'An' unless you're real careful, your heavy breathin's enough to set my finger jerkin'.'

Finn stared at the large calibre of his hideout pistol, how it was held rock steady in both of Emer's small hands. From how she'd set the action it looked like she knew how to use it.

Nonetheless the man bluffed, raised his jaw and narrowed his eyes. 'I was meanin' you work for me,' he started. 'I hired you inclusive. Don't you savvy the meanin' o' that?'

Emer shook her head briskly. 'Wrong. You hired me to sing. You said you might want me to encourage some of your customers to buy a few drinks, an' I agreed. But that's all the contract buys, Mr Finn.'

'You got someone else you're sharin' favours with, Emer?' he asked.

'No. But if an' when I do, it'll be with someone o' my choosin'. Right now all you get is to hear me sing. From someone who don't pick up on meanin's, I reckon that's clear enough.'

Lloyd Finn glowered. He wasn't used to any of his girls speaking to him in such a manner. But he hesitated to get tough because there was something about Emer that interested him. Maybe it was because she was the only person in a long time who had actually stood up to him. He made an inward smile, a concession for the trait he held a sneaky regard for.

'I ought to kick you out, put you on the Boulder City stage, you know that?'

he said as he put his shoulder holster back on.

'I expect you do, Mr Finn. But it wouldn't make much sense. You'd be losin' your singer for what, for you, would *never* be much of a jump.' Emer raised her chin defiantly, made no attempt to lower the gun or hand it back. 'How'd you explain *that* to your friends an' family?' she added with bite.

'Give me the gun,' he said, after holding her steely gaze for a second or two.

'I'll bring it to your office, just before I do my number.'

Finn didn't like it, but he smiled resignedly and nodded, grabbed his coat and started for the door. 'I trust this little ... er ... misunderstandin' stays between you an' me?' he said.

'It will if you put your coat on before you go out the door,' Emer replied.

Without another word, Finn turned the key in the lock, opened the door and went into the hallway.

As the door closed behind him, Emer

heard some coarse laughter, a response that Lloyd Finn regularly enjoyed within the comfort of his own establishment.

Emer cursed. 'Little brain, big hat,' she muttered and turned to look at her reflection in the dressing-cable mirror. If she hadn't needed the job, she *would* have taken the north-bound stage. But she was flat broke, had to keep a roof over her head while she earned some money. Besides, there was little else she could do except sing and entertain in a dance-hall. Girls with that kind of background carried a stigma; they rarely got the opportunity for reputable work, even if there was any.

Emer knew there would be trouble if she stayed. She recalled a wayside pulpit she'd once seen outside of Phoenix. 'Today's molehills are tomorrow's mountains', it had said. She bit her lip, and suppressed a sob. Then she lowered the hammer on the derringer and tossed it on to her bed. 'Yeah, you can have it later,' she said quietly.

8

It was approaching first dark when Will Fawcett and Joe Striker rode into Muletown. The low angle of the westering sun highlighted the dry potholes and erosion of the town's main street and did little to improve the look of the plain, weather-beaten buildings. Few people moved about, although there were horses at the hitchrails that appeared to run the length of the street and on both sides. The livery was in the middle of town, and inside it was gloomy and reeked of hay and horse sweat.

The indifferent liveryman told them he would grain and groom both horses and give them a stall for the night, but he demanded payment in advance. Joe paid him, and they picked up their warbags and rifles. But their way was stopped by a man who was set four-square in the double doorway.

'I got me a runner,' the man said. 'For a dollar, he gets from out o' town to my office before you get from one end o' the street to the other. Ralph Finn's the name, an' I'm your ever watchful sheriff.' Finn used his left hand to push back his hat. The shadow from the brim lifted to reveal a dark countenance with heavy features. 'Anyone stops over in Muletown has to have money in his pockets, or it's a week in the cells. That's town ordinance, an' there's no negotiatin',' he stated firmly.

'Well, we got money, Sheriff,' Will said calmly. He started to reach for the bills in his vest pocket, but stopped when he saw he was suddenly looking into the barrel of Finn's big Colt.

'Christ, you're sure a jumpy kind o' sheriff,' Will responded a tad annoyed. 'How the hell am I supposed to show you what you want to see?'

Finn said nothing, simply nodded for Will to continue.

Will showed the lawman some bills, and Joe showed the inside of Whiskey John's wallet.

The sheriff grunted and holstered his gun, but kept the palm of his hand on the butt. 'What's your names?' he asked.

'I'm Johnson an' he's Stroud,' Will lied.

'Where're you from?'

'South,' Will told him.

'Long time gone?'

'Not so long.'

The sheriff looked a little disappointed and turned his attention to Joe. 'How about you, Stroud?'

'I've drifted in from the north, Sheriff. Been a long time doin' it though.'

'Hmm, I wonder why,' Finn wondered.

Joe shrugged, but held the man's gaze. 'I wanted to see new country . . . keep on the move. Besides I'm wanted for bank robbery, an' murder an' all sorts of unruliness, along the Colorado.'

Finn curled a thick lip. 'I'll remember you said that,' he rasped. 'You boys've got enough mazula between you to choke a cow. You get paid off somewhere?'

The pair had already run through their story, and Will didn't hesitate. 'We took work at a ranch outside o' Plum Springs. But there weren't much in the way o' female company an' the boss was a devout somethin' or other an' didn't allow any gamblin'.'

'You ain't talkin' about Bradley Wallace, are you?' Finn asked.

'Hell no,' Joe said and laughed. 'We wanted to work for him, but he didn't need any more hands. No, we got fixed up with a rancher called Rote. Orville Rote.'

Finn smiled thinly. 'Yeah, I thought as much. Ol' Reborn Rote, they call him. He got religion after fallin' in a creek and gettin' bit by a whole nest o' moccasins. The son-of-a-bitch, pulled through . . . reckoned it was a sign from the Creator Himself.'

'Yeah, that's about the way we heard it,' Joe said.

'Hah, you an' every cowboy in the west knows a version o' that story.' Finn's response was wily and considered.

Joe looked towards Will and the two men smiled at how their own guile was being accepted.

'If you can recommend somewhere we can take a bath, we can rid ourselves o' this trail dust. Then, after takin' in some food, we'd like to see what your town's got to offer,' Will said.

'You're in luck, as it happens,' Finn replied. 'It's my brother who runs the Jack o' Lantern. Tell him I sent you over. He'll take care o' you . . . provide you with anythin' you want.'

'That's more'n neighbourly, Sheriff. Thank you,' Joe said.

The lawman didn't move. He just nodded, stood his ground purposefully as the two men walked around him and out of the livery.

★ ★ ★

73

By the time the two men had entered the saloon, it was well after sundown and kerosene lamps were burning around the big room. There was a lot of hanging smoke, a lot of noise from the drinkers, and a drunk sat playing an upright piano that no one was listening to. There were a few working girls, and within moments Joe had made an agreement with a curly-haired blonde. He handed the wallet of money he'd taken from Whiskey John to Will before starting up the stairs.

'Now, that ain't nice,' the girl said, stuffing a note down the front of her bodice. 'It looks like you don't trust me.'

'I'm a naturally cautious feller,' Joe said giving her elbow a nip. 'Besides, trust ain't what I'm payin you for.'

When he returned ten minutes later, he offered to take the money back while his partner sought his own feminine comforts.

Will went for a pretty, nervous-looking Mexican girl, and as they disappeared up the stairs they passed

Emer Sparrow as she was coming down. The singer was wearing a bright green dress and Will paused as his girl went on ahead.

Will touched a couple of fingers to his hat brim. 'Evenin', ma'am. Would you be workin' here tonight?' he asked courteously.

Emer's grey eyes flashed, but she took in his freshly scrubbed appearance correctly and assessed him as a new arrival in town. 'I will be in a few minutes,' she replied with a smile.

'Well, that's fine,' Will came back quickly. 'But I think I've made a mistake. Can we do a trade?' he continued awkwardly.

'Well we could, if you want a few lines o' Golden Slippers. I'm the singer here,' Emer explained shortly.

Will swiftly held up a hand. 'No offence, ma'am. I just figured wrong.'

Emer was going on down the stairs, but she stopped and looked back. 'Yeah, I know, an' I know you meant it as some sort o' compliment. Thanks anyway, cowboy.'

Will puffed his cheeks and went on up to where the girl he'd paid for stood waiting on the landing.

'You changed your mind?' she asked with a touch of offence.

'No. I was just askin' for a request,' he said appeasingly.

Meantime, downstairs, Joe watched the red-haired singer walk towards the door marked 'office'. He downed his whiskey and signalled the bartender for a refill.

'I bet she puts flavour into a feller's grub,' he said, as Emer went in through the door to Lloyd Finn's office.

'She's our canary,' the man growled. 'Trouble is, she thinks she's perched above everyone else who works here.'

'From where I'm standin', she's entitled,' Joe said approvingly.

'An' that includes you,' the bartender sneered.

Joe shrugged and snapped a dollar on to the counter. 'Leave the bottle,' he said.

In the office, Emer slid the derringer across Finn's desk. 'You left this in my room by mistake,' she said, stared unemotionally at the man before turning away.

'Stay there.' Finn rose from his chair and quickly came around the desk. 'This is empty,' he charged, picking up the gun and breaking it open.

Emer held out her left hand. Palm up, she let him see the two big cartridges. 'Stops me shootin' you,' she said. 'But I guess permissible killin' wouldn't amount to a hill o' beans with your brother.'

Finn glanced at her icily as he reached out. But instead of taking the shells, he grabbed her wrist and twisted her arm up until her hand was hard under her chin. Emer gasped as she was lifted on to her toes. Finn drew back his other hand, curled his fingers around the derringer and laughed cruelly.

'Gettin' hit with this won't improve your looks,' he rasped, breath hissing through his pinched nostrils. 'You an' me got to patch up a little misunderstandin'.'

Emer opened her mouth to yell, but Finn let go of her wrist and slapped her very fast across the front of her face. Emer fell back against the wall, a trickle of blood splitting her lip. Finn stepped forward and hit her again, then punched her low with the derringer held firm in his fist. Emer gasped, choked with pain and her knees buckled, but Finn pushed both his hands out and under her arms for support.

Still clutching the derringer he dragged her to the short sofa and let her drop. He picked up the two cartridges, loaded the gun and pushed it back into his shoulder-rigged holster. 'No more misunderstandin' an' no more nothin',' he wheezed.

Briefly paralysed by the blow to her stomach, Emer lay quiet and unmoving.

★ ★ ★

As Will came slowly down the stairs he looked around the room below, spotted Joe sitting at a corner table. As he pushed his way through the mill of customers towards his partner, the door of Finn's office crashed open and he stopped to see what the fuss was about.

Finn stood there holding the wounded Emer, his fingers sunk cruelly into her arm. She was trying to stand up and her face was red blotched, her mouth puffed and patched with blood. Finn shoved her away so roughly that she stumbled and fell awkwardly to the floor. As she kneeled there gasping and confused, one or two of the customers weren't sure whether to snigger or go to her aid. They looked to Finn who was breathing heavy, leaning against the door frame.

'You're all through here, lady. Go pack your stuff,' he rasped.

Will stepped forward and helped Emer to her feet. She fell against him, gulped air as she tried to steady herself.

'I reckon you'd have been better off

with me,' he said, and smiled reassuringly, instantly hoped she'd take it the right way.

'The story o' my life,' she slurred through painful lips. Then, muttering an appreciation for Will's help, she pushed herself away, walked shakily for the stairs back up to her room.

Finn remained in his office doorway. He was now watching Will, grinning, almost as if to garner approval. His expression didn't have time to change to surprise, before Will's fist smashed into his nose, driving him back into his office. There was an eager shout from the men who suddenly gathered around. It halted Emer at the top of the stairs and she turned to look back.

'If you're goin' to treat a lady like that, mister, I suggest you do it in private,' Will said and flexed his shoulders expectantly.

Inside Finn's office, Will took another step forward. He lashed out, back and forth across the man's face, then swung him around and grabbed him, hauled him in close. 'You don't need any more,' he hissed. 'But I reckon this earns me a few stripes with the lady.' Then he punched Finn solidly on the jaw. The blow sent the man down, crawling back across the floor of his saloon.

'No, don't. No more on my account,' Emer cried out, her voice hoarse and cracked.

As the saloon owner tried to make it to his feet, Will kicked him in the ribs. 'I'm doin' this on my account, you gutless son-of-a-bitch,' he rasped heavily.

The bartender and two of Finn's bodyguards were moving in now. But so was Joe Striker. He grabbed a chair and laid out the bartender with one almighty swinging blow. Will caught a punch on the ear. It rocked him on his feet, but he spun with the blow and managed to hook an elbow into his assailant's stomach. The man coughed. He was winded and Will followed through with a chop to the back of his neck, then a knee to the side of his head that sent him to the floor.

He turned and set himself for more, but found that Joe was getting things under control. The man who said he'd spent a long time travelling from the north, had a tight grip on the other heavy. Grabbing the man's head, he bent him near double, drove him into the zinc-edged bar. There was a gasp from the semi-circle of onlookers at the sickening thud, then another when the man crumpled to the floor and didn't move.

'You start 'em, an' I'll finish,' Joe said, and spat a gobbet of bright blood. Then he wiped his lips, looking for somewhere to rub the palms of his hands.

'Someone has to,' Will growled back, as he gently toyed with the bruising of his own face. 'Else we'd be knee-deep in all sorts o' trash.'

'Yeah, a regular pair o' rat-catchers,' a strong voice rang out.

Will and Joe turned as one, their

hands dropping towards their Colts. But they were being dealt with: they saw themselves covered by the thrusting barrel of Sheriff Ralph Finn's shotgun.

'Hello, boys,' the sheriff greeted them. 'I been checkin' my heap o' Wanted dodgers, an' it seems they got you branded as Joseph Striker an' William Fawcett. There ain't no mention o' them goddamn turkey names you laid claim to. So, if you'll just shuck them gunbelts nice an' easy, there's a jailhouse awaitin'.' The lawman's face hardened as he looked around at the now hushed crowd. 'One o' you gawpers, go fetch Doc Patterson for my brother,' he rasped.

9

Sheriff Finn used both of his jailhouse cells to lock Joe and Will in. The lawman had taken their boots, belts and hats, leaving them only their vests and pants. He also took their money and tobacco, had merely grinned when Will said he wanted a receipt.

'This money o' yours — huh, if it is *your* money — is safe enough. This is a jail goddamnit, an' I'm a goddamn lawman,' Finn told him as he walked away from the cells. He was smirking with grim satisfaction as he slammed the big, oak door behind him.

Halfway along the passage, two bitch lamps cast weak light into the cells where Joe and Will were prisoners. Joe was standing close to the iron-barred wall that divided the two cells.

'I've seen you with a gun in your mitt, but I'd never've guessed you could brawl like that,' he said.

Will laughed. 'Always keep somethin' in reserve', my pa once told me,' he replied and winced at the pain in his head. 'But did you get a look at the shotgun he was totin'? It was a goddamn Greener, an' they fire about half a pound o' lead shot. Knew a feller once, said he loaded up shoe-nails.'

'Best we backed off then,' Joe agreed. 'An' now we got ourselves a *real* little hellhole to play in.'

'Yeah, we should give some thought to what we can do about it.'

'What the hell can we do? What do you reckon your pa would have to say about it?' Joe wondered.

Will thought for a moment, then he said, 'He'd have come up with somethin' like, 'a prison's somewhere you really don't want to be, son'.'

'Yeah, he knew some good stuff,' Joe muttered, as he stepped across to his bunk. He stretched out on the spare bedding, clasped his hands behind his head and stared sullenly towards the ceiling. 'When you discover a way out, gimme a yell. If I'm not eaten by roaches,' he added.

Will said nothing as he walked slowly around his cell. He examined each bar, the lock on the door, the flagstones in the floor and under the bunk. In less than two minutes he'd found no evidence of anyone ever having made an attempt to break out. 'Likely they was too damn stove up after bein' arrested by Finn,' he said, but Joe only grunted a response.

Less than an hour later, and breaking the stifled sounds of the town's night life, the passage door swung open. The sheriff had returned and he wasn't alone. His brother was alongside him. The man's jaw was thickly padded with bandages that passed up and over the top of his head. He moved very slowly and Will guessed some bones were being held in place. In the low, greasy light, he looked grey-faced, but his eyes were burning with suppressed anger as he advanced on the cells. The bartender from the Jack o' Lantern and one of Lloyd Finn's bodyguards shuffled close behind.

Will and Joe got to their feet, cursed vehemently under their breaths when they saw, then recognized the four men. Ralph Finn held a Colt in his right hand, the keys to the cells in his left.

'Hey, Will. I reckon your pa was all mouth,' Joe suggested wryly through the separating cell bars.

'You got visitors,' Finn shouted. 'I don't usually go for such comforts, but this is a particular situation, an' I've got an' interest.'

The sheriff inserted a key in the lock on Will's door and swung it open. Will moved away from his bunk, backed off until his shoulders were against the wall. As the three men stepped into the cell he flicked his gaze between them, felt the icy run of sweat between his shoulder blades. Finn said something, but his words were low and muffled because of the bandages. Then the man lifted a hand, made an unmistakable sign and the other two advanced on Will.

'Hey, Fawcett, I nearly forgot,' the sheriff called out. 'Every time you raise a fist or a boot, I get to take a little piece out o' your partner here. His dodger says 'dead or alive', so it's no concern if he ain't delivered mint. It's up to you.'

Will hesitated, and in that moment the bartender took his advantage. He stepped in and drove a heavy fist into Will's midriff. Will gasped, bent nearly double and stumbled a pace forward. The bodyguard then took a turn and slammed a fist of iron-hard knuckles against the side of his face. He fell to his knees with his stomach aching and his head thumping with pain.

In the adjoining cell, Joe was shaking with rage. He thrust his right hand through the bars towards Finn and made a threatening fist. 'Hey, Will,' he yelled. 'I been told I got bits an' pieces on me that ain't no good anyway, so you take the cowardly scum down. I'll be all right.'

Ralph Finn raised the long barrel of his Colt, and struck Joe's fingers savagely. 'Next time I'll take 'em off,' he threatened and gave a crooked grin as Joe recoiled in agony.

Will straightened himself. He was taking a pain-filled lungful of air when the bodyguard swung a fist into his chest. The blow slammed him against the stone wall; the back of his head made a sickening crunch and lights exploded behind his eyes. As he fell forward, he saw the bartender draw back his foot, and he drew his arms in to protect himself from the man's savage kick to his side. He hit the floor and immediately rolled on to his elbows, tried to get to his knees as Lloyd Finn stepped up. The man was intending to drive the heel of his boot down into Will's face, but it was the flash and thunderous gunshot that stopped everyone from making another move.

After the resounding explosion, there was an immediate whine of the ricocheting bullet, and all the men in the cells flinched and ducked on impulse as they turned to look into the passage. Will lifted his head from the floor. He saw a blurred image of someone holding a carbine and blinked, shaking his head to clear his vision. Then he cursed with surprise when he realized it was the red-headed singer from the saloon who was standing in a drift of blue powder-smoke.

Emer Sparrow walked resolutely down the passage. Levering another round into the chamber, she kept the carbine levelled at the sheriff. As she passed the wall lamps, Will could plainly see the bruises on her face, her cut and swollen lips.

'Just let the gun drop, Sheriff,' Emer snapped out.

'Why, brother, it's your little song-bird,' the lawman retorted. 'Your dumb little songbird, who don't know the trouble she's just got herself into.'

'Just get rid of the gun,' Emer repeated.

Finn was unmoved, held his Colt down at his side. 'You drop the rifle, missy, an' we'll say no more,' he offered. 'I'll say it was a rush o' blood to your head. An' by the look o' you, that ain't too far off beam.'

For the shortest moment, Emer considered her response. 'Before I started singin' solo, me an' my pa had a double act,' she said. 'He'd hold out a double eagle, an' I'd shoot it from between his fingers, sometimes from fifty feet or more. So don't get smart *or* stupid, Sheriff. From this distance I don't even have to aim to take your head off at the neck,' she threatened coldly and without blinking.

Emer watched closely as Finn tensed. She knew as well as everyone else in the jail that he was going to try and lift his Colt, attempt a shot before she could squeeze the trigger.

But Joe was set and waiting for such a moment, had already moved so he was behind the sheriff and unsighted. He shot his left hand through the bars, grabbed the man by his neck collar and savagely jerked him back. Finn's head banged dully against the bars as Joe moved his hand down to grab at the Colt and yank it from his grip. As the man slumped down slowly, Joe cracked him over the back of his head with his own gun. Finn grunted, his mouth opened and he collapsed to the floor.

Emer swung the carbine to cover the other three men in Will's cell. Lloyd Finn's face was twisted by the anger that welled up inside him. But he blanched when he met her steely gaze. She lifted her left hand and beckoned him towards her. He snorted and shook his head while both his bartender and bodyguard looked on helplessly.

From the flagstones, Will rolled on to his back, lifted both feet and drove them violently up against Finn's backside. 'Remember who's field commander,' he rasped. Finn was propelled forwards into an uncontrol-lable stumble, regaining his balance less than a full pace from the barrel of Emer's gun.

'I'm doin' this for all the poor dumb souls who've ever worked for you, Finn,' Emer said coldly, as she angled the carbine barrel down. The colour drained from Finn's face, and Emer's expression maybe hardened a little. 'But mostly for me,' she added as she squeezed the trigger.

Finn screamed, collapsed moaning and retching as he flailed about the cell floor. The bartender and bodyguard shot their hands high in instant supplication and defeat. They clawed the air and shook their heads, no longer wanting any further part of what was happening.

As Emer surveyed her handiwork, she jacked another shell into the carbine's breech. She looked to Will who was using the bars to slowly pull himself up. By the time he'd made it, Finn had drifted into silent shock.

The sheriff sat humped on the floor, breathing heavy with his head slowly rolling from side to side. He was too hurt and nauseous to harbour any thoughts of retaliation.

'I think it's time we shook the dust out o' this miserable town, don't you?' Emer said huskily.

Will nodded. 'I think you just done that, lady,' he said. 'But if you're meanin' we take to the hills, that's fine by me.' He stepped over Finn and paused in front of the sheriff. For a moment it looked like he might dish out a closing kick, but he changed his mind, picked up the keys and walked unsteadily to Joe's cell door.

Emer forced the bodyguard and the bartender to face the wall, then made them unbuckle their gunbelts and toss them out into the passage. She prodded the sheriff with the barrel of the carbine. 'You, too. Take off your gunbelt,' she told him.

The man was still muzzy and pained, but a growl of hate returned when he saw his brother lying in a pool of blood.

Emer walked from the cell and Will

closed and locked the door.

'No one's botherin' to take a look in here tonight, Sheriff,' Will said. 'They're likely used to the sounds prisoners make when they've crossed you or your brother. Sleep well, scum sucker.'

Ralph Finn raked the two men and the girl with revengeful eyes. 'You better ride far an' fast . . . all o' you,' he gritted through the bars. 'I'll chase you down an' find you.'

In response, Joe lifted the Colt, put it through the bars and aimed it unswervingly at the sheriff's head. He actioned the hammer, held it for a few long seconds before dropping the gun to the cell's flagstones. 'Then you'll be needin' this,' he rasped and turned away.

'What the hell was that about?' Will asked.

Joe held up his gunhand. 'He busted my fingers. I want him to find me.'

It was only then that Will noticed Joe's fingers were caked with blood, realized that he'd been holding the gun in his left hand.

'I'd have shot him,' he said, immediately understanding Joe's response.

'I reckon the chase has already started, an' we ought to ride,' Emer urged impatiently after glancing at Joe's hand.

Will and Joe retrieved their boots and hats, found their guns, tobacco and money in a desk drawer, locked the jail and ran from the jailhouse. They jumped down to the hitch-rail where Emer had their horses waiting together with their saddle-bags and rifles.

'Avoid the mountains,' Emer called out obscurely, as they stowed their effects behind their saddle-bags and ridles.

'We aim to,' Will shouted back. Breathless, they swung into leather, turned and ran their mounts excitedly along the main street.

In less than a minute, a snarling pariah dog was harrying the three riders from the western end of the cowtown. Will looked around to see if there was any sign of Finn's runner, but he saw no one, unless they were hiding deep in the night shadows. A half-hour later, they hit a trail that led south towards the Gila River and the Mexican border.

10

They didn't stop until early light broke across the peaks of a distant mountain range. They'd been riding towards a slick-rock canyon that Will had heard tell of, and luckily for the worn-out riders it was just about where it was supposed to be. Emer had a look at Joe's fingers, saw that the index and middle finger on the right hand were bruised and swollen. She made splints from a mesquite to secure and protect them, while Will kept an eye on the surrounding land.

'Do you think I'll be able to use my gun again?' he asked Emer grimly.

'I'm no doctor, but I'd say probably,' she answered directly. 'But if usin' it's that important, you've got another hand,' she added.

'Glad you pointed that out, Emer, 'cause along with more trouble than we can shake a stick at, we've got the attention of half-a-dozen vultures. Makes us easy prey for them that's followin',' Will said, holding the flat of his hand against the rising sun. 'I guess we're safe enough for the moment, but we've got to consider where we're movin' on to.'

'Yeah. I'm beginnin' to think that's what some of us was put on this earth for,' Emer muttered with a glum smile.

For the next few hours, they took turns keeping guard. One of them patrolled the canyon rim while the other two slept. There were signs of dust way in the distance, but it didn't draw close enough to cause them much concern.

'I know you ain't got a hankerin' to go back south, an' I ain't goin' back north. So why not west?' Joe was putting to Will. 'I know it's California, but we'll be so deep in the country, we'll avoid trouble . . . be out o' the way o' goddamn dodgers an' stuff.'

'Are you sayin' it's somewhere there

ain't any law?' Will asked.

'It ain't much,' Joe said. 'Once met a feller who flat-boated saltfish from the Gulf to Lake Mead. He said, they make their own. If we head for Yuma, we can decide when we get there. If you don't like it, we can stay in Arizona, or ride straight on into Mexico. What do you say?'

Will shrugged. 'Yeah, I guess. It's still a hell of a ride. How about you, Emer?' he asked.

Poking at the small camp-fire, Emer looked from one man to the other. 'Do you reckon they need singers?' she asked with a wry smile.

'Yeah,' Joe confirmed readily. 'That same fish feller told me saloons are cryin' out for 'em. Need 'em like bears needs honey, he said.'

'Then I guess it's Yuma,' Emer said, retaining her smile. 'But don't do anythin' or go anywhere just 'cause o' me. I broke you out o' that jail 'cause of what you did for me at the Jack o' Lantern. I can look after myself wherever you fetch up.'

Will nodded, gave a crooked grin. 'Yeah, OK, an' I do know of a trail that should get us past any regulators or lawmen who might still be patrollin' these parts.'

'Have you been to Yuma before?' Joe asked Will.

'Close. A couple o' days' ride to cross the Gila. Some time back, I rode with a wild bunch o' mavericks down from San Bernardino. What you thinkin'?'

Joe looked uncertain, hesitant. 'Nothin', maybe somethin'. I heard they were handin' out parcels o' land. An encouragement for settlers.'

'Yeah, I'd heard that,' Will said, giving Joe a curious look.

Joe twisted his mouth into a grin. 'I figured you'd be interested.'

Again Will shrugged. 'The thought ain't that far away. I've drifted for too long, an' that trouble in Muletown didn't help. So, yeah, could be I'm ready to put down some roots.'

'Hell, you sound a tad serious . . .

like a goddamn turnip or somethin',' Joe returned.

Will nodded. 'Maybe I am. This sort o' life ain't goin' to get me enough dollars to buy a stump farm, even. Much longer an' all the free land'll be gone, or in the hands o' goddamn scalpers.'

'As long as it's west o' the Rockies, there'll always be *somewhere* you can prove-up on,' Joe said easily. 'Personally though, I want to journey while I'm young, an' that's now. I'm for makin' a good-lookin' corpse.'

'I bet the dumbcluck you heard say that's dead by now,' Emer said sharply.

'It was *me* said it,' Joe protested. A moment later, the three of them laughed cheerily.

Joe turned to Emer. 'You'll only make trouble for yourself by stickin' with us, even if Will is only diggin' taters,' he said. 'Hah, I mean, you weren't plannin' to stay in Muletown for ever, were you?'

'No. Then I'll probably never make it

to the big Eastern show palaces either. I'll find somewhere to sing — saloons, dance halls, a small town theatre, even. Most folk on the frontier seem to like what I do.'

'It's a risky sort o' life for a young, good-lookin' woman who's on her own,' Will said.

'Thanks for that, Will,' Emer replied and laughed again. 'But it's not so bad if you can see it comin'.'

'Like you did with Lloyd Finn,' Joe suggested.

Emer's smile disappeared and she nodded curtly. 'I guess there's always an exception. My husband was fine-looking, but that was about all. I married him very young, but he was even younger. He missed out on part of his life — well, the gamblin' part — an' it didn't take him long to do somethin' about it. He started ridin' the rails back an' forth between Flagstaff an' Gallup. He played poker an' bones . . . said that one day he'd find enough spots to make us a fortune. Huh, the only thing he ever made was me a poor widow. So I guess you don't always learn, either.'

'That's somethin' could be said o' most folk,' Will commiserated.

'One day he never came back. I knew as much, but it still came as a bit of a kick in the teeth. I didn't have any money, so I asked a saloon owner if I could sing for whatever the customers threw my way. He agreed. It took the starch out o' the town's busybodies o' course, but I had no choice. Singin' was just about all I could do.'

'What about *him* . . . your husband?' Will asked, with pronounced displeasure.

'He got himself knifed in an argument. Unfortunately for him, the train was on a trestle bridge crossing the Little Colorado. Our marriage was well over by then though, an' I couldn't afford to wear weeds even if I'd wanted to.'

Emer stopped talking and looked a little uncomfortable. It was the first time she'd explained to anybody how she came to be working in saloons, and somehow she found herself wanting Joe and Will to understand her predicament, particularly Will.

'Sparrow, more or less says what you do. Is it your real name?' Will asked with a dry smile.

'No. My real name didn't look right on a saloon's billboard. So when someone told me I sounded like a songbird, I thought I'd be one. 'Cept sparrows ain't rightly songbirds.'

'Hah, you're lucky it was someone who appreciated you,' Will retorted.

During the day they'd still seen no sign of any following posse, and they quit the canyon while it was still light. They rode through a valley that cut the Chocolate Mountains, then continued due south in the direction of Mexico.

11

Out on the brush flats, not everything was as it appeared. There was a posse, but it had split up, some riding hard through the mountain's timbered slopes. From a stand of old juniper, a rider from the group had spotted the trio and triggered two quick shots into the air. But the signal had warned the fugitives too, and they changed direction, broke into a run for more rugged terrain, somewhere with hard-going and shelter.

Against the lowering sun they saw the dust clouds, the two sections of the posse closing in on them in a pincer-like movement. Joe led the way through timber that was so dense in places it slowed them to a cautious walk, but eventually they came out on a grass-covered slope above a tributary of the Gila River.

'Yeah, we can ride on till it meets the Colorado, then it's clear to Yuma,' Will told them. 'The Mexico border's about another day's ride.'

'If they're goin' to miss us here, won't they cut the river downstream . . . take cover an' just wait for us?' Joe wanted to know.

'Not if we get there first, they won't. Let's go.'

Joe rode his mount down the slope, and the animal whickered violently as its feet slithered one way then another. But Joe was a good horseman and, using skill and strength, he arrived at the bottom of the slope without much difficulty.

'Ain't all that difficult. Just stick with me, an' remember your horse don't want to fall,' Will said, and gave Emer a reassuring grin when she looked to him in alarm. Then he whipped off his hat, slapped it across the rump of her chestnut mare and called for his own mount to move off. They went down side by side struggling to stay in the saddle, both horses snorting with alarm and excitement.

At the bottom of the slope, they plunged into the river. Joe was already swimming his mount downstream with the current. Will slipped from the saddle and clung to the horn, glancing across at Emer. She was obviously petrified at the thought of doing the same to swim alongside her horse. He dragged his mount in close to hers and reached up to bend his free arm around her waist. She fought to resist, to stay in the saddle, but he prised her fingers loose and pulled her into the river. She went under for a moment, came up blinking and spluttering, flailing her arms.

'My dance,' Will yelled. Then he grabbed one of her wrists, forced her hand to the saddle horn while still clutching his own with the other. Emer's fingers grasped it and she held tight, took a few calming breaths.

The current was steady and carried them downstream at a good rate. After they'd all been in the water for an interminable half-hour, Joe, who was well ahead, drew his mount on to a stony bar that was separated from the bank by a strip of calm water only a few feet wide. A few minutes later, Will and Emer followed suit. They left the river, led their mounts up and into a mesquite brake that grew right to the edge of the water. For some time, Will helped Joe to cover their tracks. They replaced the disturbed vegetation so that anyone following would have trouble finding just where they'd quit the river. Then, shivering and wet, they rode into the closing darkness.

Late that night they made coldharbour camp on the rise of a hogback, and in the grey early light of dawn, Will pointed out the buildings of a distant town.

'So that's Yuma, eh?' Joe said. 'Stuffed full o' laws an' lawmen.'

'You were informed there weren't any,' Will reminded him.

'Yeah, but maybe the feller lied.'

'Shouldn't ever trust a goddamn fisherman,' Will said. 'Either way, we have to have supplies. What little grub we had's now a tad damp.'

'I can ride in an' see how the land lies. I've got somethin' in my saddle-bags I can wear,' Emer suggested helpfully. 'No one's goin' to look twice at a girl payin' cash an' wearin' homespuns,' she said, holding out her hand for some dollars.

An hour later, Emer was in Yuma. She circled the town, entered from the west, through what appeared to be a residential area with two-storey houses and picket fences. She tethered her horse at a post beside a dried-up water fountain, walked on to where stores and offices lined the wide, main street.

By mid afternoon she had returned with a sack of food, coffee and tobacco and a small sheaf of papers.

'You have any trouble?' Will asked, the concern showing on his face.

'Not really. I was a face among many. But the storekeeper did say he didn't remember seein' me around. I kept a straight face an' said I'd been ill. He gave me a funny look, but seemed to accept it.'

'You said, 'not really'. So what else was there?' Will continued.

Emer frowned. 'They've got a marshal's office right in the middle o' town. Him, or one of his deputies was sittin' outside, so I didn't go up for a look. But a couple o' dodgers they'd got posted was for you an' Joe . . . I didn't hang around to see if there was anythin' with *my* likeness.'

'So we head on to the Mexico line,' Joe said. 'That's what we said we'd do, if we didn't like the look o' somethin'.'

'I guess,' Will conceded. 'Goddamnit, I'd already settled on gettin' a slice o' that homestead land.' He held up the paper Emer had brought back. 'Emer brought me back this,' he said, and held up a handbill with details of the offer. It was for a full section of land that was there for the taking, provided the settler made improvements within six months, and as laid down by State administration.

'No amount o' free land's any good, if they're only goin' to bury you on it,' Joe offered, looking at Emer for support.

'Like Will, I'd rather it was California,' she said. 'With new towns springin' up, there'd be a lot more opportunities for me. But Joe's right. This ain't the time for any of us to push their luck here. So I guess it's south. Unless you want to split up. Maybe that'll be safer. They are lookin' for a gang o' three ... two men an' a woman.'

'It's a thought, but I don't reckon there's any need for that right now,' Will decided.

'Yeah, maybe we should see what chow the lady brought back,' Joe said.

12

Hiding out by day, riding by night, the riders made their way towards the Arizona-Mexico border.

There were posses abroad, not necessarily hunting Will, Joe and Emer, but they were lawmen nonetheless; resolute deputies who were suspicious of just about every rider whose trail they crossed. 'Not that far from killers 'emselves', was Joe's opinion of the so-called peace officers. They were to learn later, there'd been a big railroad robbery west of Tucson. An inter-state manhunt ensued and it was funded by the company's owners who hired tough, professional Pinkerton agents.

For a while it made it risky for the trio to move about, for anyone who operated on the edge of the law. To add to their troubles, a wet norther blew in and marooned them in the wildest country for four days. At the very edge of the Gila Desert, flash floods filled dry washes and gulches, turning them into impassable, turbulent rivers.

They holed up in a shallow cavern where Emer shortly found herself the centre of attention. With the rain forcing them into more intimate con-tact, she became aware of a developing rivalry for her attention. All of a sudden, neither Joe nor Will wanted to go out alone to search for firewood or anything else they needed. They were obviously reluctant to leave the other with her, and she had to browbeat them into going together.

There were moments when Emer enjoyed the play for her attention, but she knew it could become a treacherous adversary. It was the night the rain stopped — when they decided to move out the following morning — that the trouble she'd been hoping to avoid, became very real.

Emer decided to use up the last of their food on a more fulsome meal. It would be their last until they obtained more supplies, and she asked both men to hunt for extra firewood. Since they had camped, they had used up what was readily available, and the men were forced to collect from slightly further afield.

Emer was hacking at the joints of a cottontail, when Joe suddenly reappeared. Ducking through the cavern's low entrance, he was carrying a handful of light kindling and a few sticks of brushwood.

'Is that all you could find?' she asked cheerily, but with a shade of unease.

'Yeah,' he said, dropping them into the pile of warm ash. 'Well, it was about all I looked for,' he added. 'I got to thinkin' there must be better things in life.'

'There are, Joe, but there's a time an' a place for everythin',' she said, speculating on what was about to happen.

As she turned away to hide her worried look, Joe lifted his left arm, put his hand around the top of her shoulder, his thumb on the back of her neck.

'Stop that, Joe,' she said, with a small gasping laugh. 'It ain't like you got cabin fever or anythin'.'

'I sure got somethin', Emer,' he replied, lowering his arm to her waist and moving in close behind her. 'I ain't goin' to hurt you, you know that.' His voice was hoarser now when he spoke. 'I been watchin' you . . . how you move about. Either you're real dumb, Emer — which you sure as hell ain't — or you been waitin' for this, same as me.'

'I'm sorry, Joe, but all I'm waitin' for is to get out o' this goddamn place. Now let me go, before Will gets back,' she answered back, unmoving and as chilly as she could muster.

'He won't be here for ages. He'll have to go clear over the ridge to find anythin' good enough for burnin'. 'An' I don't think you're for sharin', Emer. I weren't meanin' anythin' like that. Will don't have to know.'

'Goddamnit, Joe, there's nothin' for him *to* know.' Emer turned, and she felt Joe's hold relax a little. She tried an innocent smile, brought the stub-bladed knife she'd been using up under Joe's chin. 'Please don't spoil things, Joe,' she said, 'not while I'm still holding this.' Then she gave a violent twist that broke his grip, and shoved him away.

Joe grunted with surprise, and immediately started towards her. He made a grab for her wrist, missed and tried again as she brandished the knife back at him. Then he stopped, suddenly let her go when he sensed they weren't alone any more.

'That's it, Joe, don't go spoilin' things,' Will called out calmly, 'or I'll have to blow your goddamn head off, so help me.' Will was standing just inside the entrance to their cavern, and his Colt was pointing straight between Joe's eyes.

Emer had turned pale. 'Will . . . it's all right . . . ' she started tensely.

'You want I should go back for more wood?' he suggested, his voice brittle.

'No, please,' she exclaimed. 'There's nothin' goin' on. I don't want any trouble. Joe was just foolin'.'

Will took a step forward, looked into Emer's suffering face for a long moment before turning to Joe. 'Is that what you call it, Joe . . . just foolin'?'

'What else, Will?' Joe said, his eyes bright and challenging. 'What else *could* a one-armed feller be doin'?'

'It ain't your goddamn arm I'm worried about,' Will snapped back. Then he lowered his gun, shoved it back into its holster.

'That's better,' Joe said, and poked the splinted fingers of his right hand at Will. 'But next time, don't you go pointin' a gun at me,' he warned.

Will held his demanding gaze. 'If there is a next time, Joe, I might not let Emer stop me from usin' it.'

Emer forced a nervous laugh and stepped between them. 'C'mon, you two,' she said, 'we can make do with the

118

bits o' wood we've got. Get the fire goin', an' I'll fetch some water. We've got hot meat an' biscuits an' canned peaches an' coffee with sugar.'

Emer knew she'd warded off trouble. It was by a hair's breadth, and she knew it could flare up again. She'd seen the look not only from Joe, but in the eyes of other men. The sooner they were back in the saddle with their minds on the trail ahead, the better and safer they'd be, she thought.

The three of them packed what was left of their provisions and left the shelter of the cavern just before first dark.

For another full day they rode and eventually approached a one-horse, mongrel town that sat on the very edge of the border between Arizona and Mexico.

Emer decided on her tactic of riding in to check on the situation. At one end of a shallow, rock-strewn gully, she left Will and Joe sitting beneath the spread of a gnarled oak.

'Try to stay away from each other's throats,' were her considered words of advice as she rode off.

Minutes later, and as if in response, Joe unwound the binding and removed the splint from his fingers. 'Goddamn fingers need to have air an' exercise,' he said. 'Put us back on equal terms, eh?' he said artfully.

But Will had something else on his mind and disregarded Joe's taunt. 'Have you taken a real shine to Emer, or were you just feelin' horny back there?' he asked.

Joe frowned. Any other time he would have laughed off Will's question, made some wisecrack reply. But right at that moment he wasn't in the mood for being questioned. 'None o' your god-damn business,' he growled, looked up from where he'd started to clean his Colt.

Will finished building a cigarette, struck it between his lips and fumbled for a moment in his shirt pocket. 'You carryin' matches?' he asked.

'Find your own goddamn light.'

Will laughed and shook his head. 'Have I touched on somethin'?' he bounced back. 'I was only askin' 'cause I've taken somethin' of a fancy to her myself. I didn't want you as any sort o' rival.'

Joe got to his feet. His features tightened. 'If I've got feelin's for Emer, it's for me to know . . . maybe her. Not you,' he rasped. 'You understand?'

Will became a tad more wary. He removed the unlit cigarette from his mouth and gave Joe a thoughtful look. 'Yep, I understand. It ain't an answer though. Maybe I'll ask later when you ain't so spooky,' he said.

Joe thumbed open the cylinder of his Colt, looked at and checked each of the cartridges. 'I wouldn't,' he advised coldly. 'Else you really will have me as a rival.'

Will cursed under his breath. 'I know you got a busted hand, Joe. It's put you in a black mood an' you're spoilin' for a fight, but — '

'*Did have*,' Joe broke in intolerantly. '*Did have* a busted hand, so don't go forgettin' it.'

It was clear now that Will had touched a very raw nerve. 'OK, Joe, if that's the way you want it,' he relented. 'Let's forget Emer, just pretend I said somethin' else you didn't like. I'm goin' to take a look around . . . make friends with a prickly pear.'

As Will got up to move away, Joe stuck out his leg. It tripped Will, sent him stumbling forwards awkwardly.

'Clumsy son-of-a-bitch. Steppin' out like some locoweeded cow,' Joe goaded.

Will steadied himself, realized Joe had to get something out of his system and that a fight was inevitable. As he was wondering how to handle it, Joe was already coming at him. He swung his arm, was aiming to gunwhip him with the barrel of his loaded gun. Will quickly ducked, swerved his body aside and slammed a fist into Joe's stomach. It wasn't a fully muscled punch, and Joe gasped and clawed at Will with his free hand, reached up to grab a handful of hair. But he couldn't gain a grip, and Will yanked his head free, slammed the knuckles of his fist hard into Joe's gunhand.

Joe dropped the Colt, and Will immediately hit him in the chest, ran him back and up against the bole of the oak. He moved up close, breathing heavily, looked hard into the man's smouldering eyes.

'Quit it, Joe. You've gone far enough with this,' he hissed. 'It ain't my fault that Finn smashed your fingers, or that you've got an appetite for Emer. Soon there's likely goin' to be others you an' me got to go up against, not each other.'

With that, Will eased the pressure, took a guarded step back. Joe squeezed his eyes with pain, coughed and rubbed his chest. Anger and hurt was etched deep across his face as he glared at Will. Abruptly, he shouldered him aside, picked up his Colt and rammed it into his holster. Then he dusted off his hat and shaking with bitterness stomped off along the gully.

Later, after Will had found some matches in his saddle pockets and was smoking his cigarette, he heard the not-too-far-away sound of gunfire. It was Joe using his injured hand to practise with his Colt, and Will cursed. He hoped the shots wouldn't bring any unwanted attention, but he didn't feel like telling him to quit. Things were going to be greatly strained for a while, he reckoned. Joe Striker wasn't the sort of man to let much time go by before settling a score. Will decided if there was another chance to speak, he'd suggest they split up before one of them got badly hurt.

13

There were hardly a dozen buildings in Alto Rapina, and Cable's store was the biggest. It was a general store and saloon combined with a pair of swing half-doors leading from one half to the other. Upstairs, Walter Cable had rooms he rented to anyone unlucky enough to be stranded overnight, itinerant drummers, maybe the occasional border jumper.

The town didn't run to a full time sheriff. Cable served as a sort of magistrate in minor disputes, had been known on more than one occasion to take Sunday Service at the small, white-walled church.

Among the other buildings were a run-down livery and grain store, and an adobe cantina with a screen door. Into the rear wall was built a small cube-like building of heavy, chinked logs, a solid door with an iron strap across its narrow window. It was the calaboose, the town's rudimentary jailhouse.

Unassuming and quiet, like when she approached Yuma, Emer rode in through random stands of plum and black walnut trees. But straight off, she felt the stares of the few townsfolk who were about. For evident reason, she was tense inside as she made her way along the single street to the store. It was a long time since she'd been in a town that appeared to resent strangers; she wondered if there was some particular reason for it.

Well, she wouldn't be here for long, so let the thought trail off as she passed by the old livery. Although there were only a few stalls, she saw they were full, with other mounts, some mules, tethered to a running rail in the aisle. 'Just my luck to hit town during poke-a-pig week,' she muttered wryly.

When she came to Cable's store, Emer counted ten horses crowding the hitch rail outside. Some showed signs of having been ridden hard and far, and the rising anxiety she felt inside suddenly became a big, solid knot. She could hear the noise coming from the saloon part of the store, wondered if the owners of all the horses she'd seen were the drinkers. By their rigging, some of them at the rail could belong to a posse, Arizona Rangers, renegade Mexican soldiers even.

Emer felt there was something wrong. She had an urge to turn and run, but it was too late. Too many folk had already seen her and all she could do now, was to act as naturally as possible. She tethered her mare alongside a branded buckskin, then pulled a gunny sack from her saddle-bags.

Walter Cable was a big man with an apron tied about his vast belly. A couple of townswomen were standing in the store gossiping, and they paused to stare, as Emer's entrance pinged the bell above the front door.

'Good mornin', ma'am. Can I be o' help?' Cable asked, nodded politely as

Emer approached the counter.

Well, that's friendly enough, Emer thought, trying to allay her feelings of unease. She had to raise her voice because she was fighting against both losing it, and the noise issuing from the saloon.

'I'd like to buy some provisions,' she said, turning towards the store's inner batwings, and frowning.

Cable grunted, walked over to the doors and shouted for the men to make less noise. 'Hey, you fellers, shut your noise. There's a lady here tryin' to do her marketin'.'

'Sorry, ma'am,' Cable apologized, fully aware that his call didn't have any effect on those men drinking. 'Boys have come in from a hard trail. They got a lot o' dust to cut.'

'An' traildrivers don't have a better nature to appeal to,' Emer said, returning an understanding smile.

Cable laughed. 'No, ma'am, that's posse noise . . . some Pinkertons too. They've been huntin' the train bandits.

You know, them who hit the Pacific Flyer.'

Emer didn't know, and telling another storekeeper she'd been poorly, was stretching it. But it sounded as though the robbery must be general knowledge, so she smiled again and nodded. 'I guess me an' my husband will be in later to order up proper,' she said and told the man what it was she'd come in for.

'Do I know your husband?' Cable enquired.

Emer was ready with a bogus line. 'Abe? You might've seen him. He's only been in a couple o' times. We've recently taken up some homestead land,' she responded.

'Oh yeah? Beyond Orange Butte?'

'That's right. Where the river bends,' she continued with her short yarn.

'Well you ain't too far from regular folk. Not that you can call all of us that,' Cable suggested amiably.

Emer made an agreeable noise. 'It's far enough to get lonely,' she said. 'I'll have a bacon haunch, an' a couple o' cans o' peaches, if you got 'em. My Abe loves 'em . . . eats 'em off the same plate, would you believe?'

'Ha! There's no accountin' for taste, ma'am. If you want, I got flour an' butter, Arbuckle's coffee. You can save good money by orderin' a quantity. Most folk do,' Cable offered.

Emer shook her head. 'No, thank you. I just want the things I said.'

'Well, that sure don't add up to much.' Cable frowned as he looked at the items he was putting on the counter. 'Looks more like trail grub.' He saw Emer wasn't going to respond and he shrugged. 'But I guess you know your needs better'n me,' he added, his tone a little less friendly.

While he was totting up the cost, the batwings opened and a man holding an empty beer glass in one hand, stepped through.

'Hey, a feller could die o' thirst through here,' he called out.

'I'll be right with you.' Cable smiled

unconcernedly as he handed Emer the slip of paper.

As she dug out the money, Emer fumbled and dropped some coins. She was flustered because she'd recognized the man she'd seen sitting outside of the marshal's office in Yuma.

14

From way along the gully, the sporadic gunfire continued. But Will still didn't really want to find Joe; to tell him he'd better stop in case the sound brought someone out to investigate. Then from the east, his attention was drawn to what looked like dust rising in the distance. He climbed the scrub-sided defile, watched until he saw that the small disturbances were definitely moving closer.

Will wasn't ready to presume it was Emer returning, and ten minutes later he found Joe. The man was crouching with his back to him, his right hand a few inches from the butt of his Colt. He started to draw just as Will took a step towards him. He got the gun out fast enough, but fumbled as he attempted to trigger off a shot. When he turned and saw Will, his face flushed and continuing resentment showed in his eyes.

'Askin' for a bullet sneakin' up on a man like that,' he rasped. 'How long you been standin' there?'

'No time at all, Joe. Perhaps long enough to see you got a problem,' Will said holding up his hand. 'I just came to tell you there's a rider headed this way. It looks like there's only one of 'em, but it might be best if you hang fire on that practice shootin' till we find out.' Then he gestured to the Colt. 'If them fingers are givin' you real trouble, try fannin' the hammer. It can be pretty effective in a scrape.'

'Yeah, aim at a gopher an' kill a cow,' Joe snapped back, still prickly that Will had seen his ineptness. 'What use am I goin' to be when that goddamn sheriff catches up with us . . . the one who said he'd chase us down?' Joe held up his crooked fingers and cursed Ralph Finn.

'You should've shot him,' Will replied. 'Anyway, stop makin' so much noise. It's likely Emer who' comin', but we can't be sure.'

'Since when are you the boss o' this outfit?' Joe continued angrily.

'Hell, man, I ain't bossin' you. Just think for a second. What if that rider ain't Emer? If it's a scout from some goddamn posse, you'll have led 'em straight here.'

While Will was talking, Joe was only half listening. He was more intent on pulling his Colt in and out of its holster. He kept shaking his head, obviously not satisfied with his movement or grip. Frustration was twisting his face, his jaw muscles working when he glared back at Will.

'If it is, I'll need to use a gun. Can't you goddamn well see that?' Joe cursed him and drew his Colt once again. Will flinched as the man grimaced and got off two, fast shots. The bullets went wide of their target of a prickly pear, ricocheted off stony ground not far beyond. Will immediately leaped forward and grabbed the Colt, wrenched it viciously from Joe's hand.

Joe roared with a potent mix of pain and rage as one of his bad fingers caught in the trigger guard. When Will tossed the gun aside, he charged, slammed a hard left into the side of Will's face, swung wildly with his elbows and brought his knee up savagely.

Will gasped. He turned his leg in time to take the blow, but wilted under the ferocity of Joe's surprise attack. He raised his forearms for cover, ducked and weaved his head from side to side. Then he was able to ram his head forward into Joe's face, forcing him to stagger back. It gave Will the chance he needed to step away from the boulder and get some room to manoeuvre.

'What the hell are you doin, Joe?' Will rasped out. 'You know I can knock the wad out o' you. For Christ's sake, back off.'

But Joe came back, growling and with fists sledging. Will held up his hand to stop an awkward right, heard Joe suck in a sharp breath as he hurt his injured fingers again. But now Will was getting angry, knew he had to somehow stop the fight for both their own good. He parried another blow, pushed Joe's arm aside and drove a hard right, low into his face. Then he hit him again, and blood instantly spattered, flowed from the man's smashed nose. Staggering to stay upright, Joe went back on shaky legs and Will stalked him. He slammed one more punch into his belly, took a step back as Joe crumpled to the ground.

Joe rolled, stretched out his left hand in search of his Colt. Will's face registered instant shock as he realized Joe was getting his gun back, would use it now to try and kill him.

Will made off for the cover of a big old cactus as Joe's Colt crashed out. A bullet pulsed inches from his head as he drew his own gun, turned and levelled it on Joe. 'Hell, Joe,' he yelled, watched in blunted torment as the man steadied himself for another shot. 'I don't want this. You're makin' me kill you, for Chris'sakes.'

But Emer had made it back. 'Stop it. Stop it, you damn fools!' she cried out from her weary mare. 'I've been followed most o' the way from town. Now all that gunfire's goin' to lead 'em right here.'

Will kept his eye on Joe as he holstered his Colt. Both men stared incredulously at Emer, but it was Will who spoke first. 'Lead who here?' he said, thinking it was the most important thing to reply with.

'A posse o' some sort. There's one of 'em must've rode from Yuma,' Emer answered breathlessly. 'They were in the store . . . drinkin' in the next room. There's too few folk around here for 'em not to be interested when a stranger turns up. They must've got suspicious an' said somethin'.'

Will snatched up his hat, wiped the back of his sleeve across his bleeding mouth. 'If there's riders on the way, we can't stay here. We'll make a three-way split,' he stated.

'Do we meet up again?' Emer asked.

Will hesitated, took a quick look at Joe's grim face before shaking his head. 'I guess not, Emer. The day's been fast comin' for us to make our own way.' He walked toward Joe, held out his right hand. 'Divide an' conquer, eh, Joe?' he quipped.

Joe nodded brusquely, but didn't shake hands. 'Yeah. I never was much for rubbin' along,' he muttered, gave Will a thin, unreadable look.

Emer had untied one of her saddlebags, was pulling out some of the supplies she'd bought in Alto Rapina. As they hurried back to where the horses were tethered, she handed out cans and small packages to the two men.

'If our paths cross, maybe you'll hear me singin',' she said, barely raising a smile.

'No doubt that'll be next time I'm passin' one o' them big, Eastern theatres,' Will said, as he swung into the saddle. He was going to say something further, but seemed to change his mind. 'How far behind are they . . . those lawmen?' he asked.

'They'll be here shortly.'

'Then we'll ride out through the end of this draw,' Will recommended.

Without a further word, Joe, who'd been sitting his saddle surly, dragged his horse around, dug his spurs and sent it racing north.

Will shrugged, cursed quietly. 'Someone can expect trouble,' he muttered.

'What happened here?' Emer asked, moving her mount forward.

'Joe got mad 'cause he can't use his gun like he used to. I was the dupe.'

'I was thinkin' it might have been somethin' to do with me,' Emer suggested drily.

Will looked into her eyes as he rode alongside. 'You might've had a mention,' he said. Then suddenly, he made up his mind about what it was he wanted to say. 'Look, Arizona's the devil Joe knows, an' I reckon that's where he'll go back to. If that posse do follow, they'll expect us to do the same.'

Emer nodded, looked interested.

'What are you sayin'?' she asked.

'I'm for headin' north too, but into California . . . across the Colorado.'

'What then?'

'Stay clear o' trouble, an' have a look at them parcels o' homestead land. If not, I'll ride on. There's a feller named Reborn Rotes . . . gives work to them who transgress.'

'Are you serious? Is that *really* what you want to do?' Emer asked uneasily.

'It could be, Emer. Specially if you were to come along,' Will proposed.

Emer didn't respond, kept her thoughts to herself as they rode Indian file from the gulch they'd been holed up in. When they headed on to the plain, they could see no sign of Joe. But a wisp of dust hung in the air to the north and junco finches flitted in the tops of low manzanita.

'Yeah, he's headed back towards the Gila. I hope he makes it,' Will said, and turned to Emer. 'Well, do you want to make a try of it with me?' he put to her again.

Emer smiled kindly. 'That's some invitation, Will, an' I sure appreciate the offer . . . been thinkin' about it too. But I really don't want to go beyond the next town we come to, wherever that is.'

Will sniffed, then nodded in an attempt to conceal his regret. A few moments later, Emer continued, 'I don't mind workin' in a town at the back o' beyond. I think maybe it's a way to start over, an' on my own, if you know what I mean.'

'Yeah, I guess I do,' Will replied, hoping he didn't sound as disappointed as he felt. 'Well, anyway the offer's always open . . . probably will be until this time tomorrow,' he added with a thin smile. 'If you ever do decide to take me up on it, come lookin' for someone callin' himself Johnson. He'll more'n likely have a long beard an' a bent back.' Then with his smile faded, he added a more serious note. 'Remember to look out for the next Lloyd Finn. There will be one.'

'I know,' Emer said with a swift nod.

'You're a good man, Will Fawcett. If I hadn't forgotten how, I'd pray you find what it is you're lookin' for. Meantime, you got food to last a couple o' days. After that, you're on your own.'

Will touched his hatbrim, then, looking beyond Emer, held his hand out as a sign for them to listen.

Across the great press of silence, they could hear distant shouting, the whinnying of protesting horses as chasing horsemen rode into the far end of the dry gulch.

Emer smiled as a goodbye gesture, touched heels to her mare and started to ride dead west.

Will turned his horse and rode the border line towards California. Not intending to cover his tracks, he wanted to lead the posse after him and away from Emer. 'Follow me, why don't you?' he called out. 'Let's see how good you are.'

15

Joe Striker was still seething as he drove his horse from scrubby timber on to the rock-studded desert. He knew he'd be exposed to a following posse, but there was no other choice. He had to cross arid desert land to get to the Gila River, hope that his horse would remain fleet enough to keep him a jump or two ahead of his pursuers.

As he rode, he considered his regret for turning on Will. When he discovered he could only handle his Colt like an arthritic old roper, Will was the one who was around for him to vent his spleen on. Still, when or *if* he got the chance, he'd try moving on Will's suggestion of fanning the hammer. Christ, he thought, if he did it properly, he'd frighten the population of most border towns half to death. But on reflection, it bothered him that the few gunnies who'd run with a reputation for that particular method of gunplay, were long dead.

But first he had to shake out from the posse, or whatever gang the chasing riders belonged to. He glanced behind, saw the dust they raised as they raced from the gully. He knew it wasn't Emer's fault, even though in a curious way he wanted to blame her. She'd ridden hard from Alto Rapina, and he cursed at himself when he thought that she could have headed off anywhere, instead of riding to warn him and Will, let alone bring them food. And he'd genuinely taken a fondness to her. Maybe not as strongly as Will, but if the three of them had stayed together, there's no doubt there would have been more fighting for her attention. Well, that was about it, he concluded. He'd made a few wrongs, perhaps one day he could put them to rights.

Although more trouble was closing in on him, Joe realized there was a certain vicarious thrill out of riding the wild, owl-hoot trail — like adding a big pinch of chilli to a bowl of beef and potato stew. During the last few years he'd tried his hand at outlawry, more than once speculated on whether he could succeed at it. But as of right now, having to run a weary horse all the way to Buckeye or Phoenix, even, was a way of life that bull-dogged his destination. The prospect of losing himself in the hustle and bustle of a civilized town was also bizarre, but it dragged out a grim smile.

He managed to stay ahead of the posse until dark, but they were closer now, pursuing him with grinding determination. He thought they might be planning on bringing him in dead, so they could hang the Pacific Flyer job on him. If they hadn't had any success in finding those bandits who'd actually carried out the raid, they'd likely settle for whoever they could get. He sure wouldn't be in much of a position to argue, and it would gain them a big dollar bonus.

The thought sent a shiver through him, and although his horse was ready to drop, he didn't dare rest up simply because the sun had westered. Ahead of him was a hundred-mile ridge of giant, flat-topped mesas, but he remembered Will saying that if you didn't, or *couldn't*, head west and ride around them, there *were* ways through — fissures in the rock through which it was possible to lead a horse up, then over. If he could find one of them and cross during the night, chances were he'd find himself within spitting distance of the Gila. I wonder if I'm ever goin' to cross that river without someone snappin' at my goddamn hide, he wondered.

He dismounted and for an hour led the protesting animal up into the rocky mesa. He couldn't hasten his flight because of the darkness, and the trail was narrow, perilous underfoot with loose scree.

The moon rose earlier than he had expected and, moving with very little natural cover, it was inevitable that someone in the posse below would spot him. The first hail of gunfire crashed through the hills, chipping away at the edge of the trail as bullets spat and whined around him. He could see the dark shapes of half-a-dozen horsemen way below and he cursed. Now they'd spotted him, they'd discover the trail he was using and he'd wanted to be way gone before that happened. He cursed again, but from his vantage point he figured he could retaliate, at least slow them down. He moved around his horse, pulled his rifle from its scabbard and knelt with his back to the wall of the mesa. Aiming generally at some place within the group, he got off three shots. The lead buzzed and smacked off the rocky ground, and one man's horse squealed in fear, reared up and threw its rider from the saddle.

'Should set some bees buzzin',' Joe grunted in quiet satisfaction. Another horse caught the shock and jumped around causing more chaos. Joe added to the confusion by firing off his remaining shots. 'Shouldn't be so keen to chase me now,' he added coolly.

After a minute or two's watching, he hurried back up the narrow track to his horse that had steadily kept moving. Another fifteen minutes and he'd made his way around a long crook of the mesa wall. It brought the end of the rocky trail that much closer, but he had to do something to make them think further pursuit was futile. If he didn't, they'd continue to hunt him down, and he had to do it before they had sorted themselves out, while he was still unsighted.

If he'd had a spare mount, he would have sacrificed it. But he didn't and needed the horse he had, fatigued though it was.

'*Adios* to forty dollars,' he muttered, as he removed the saddle. He kept the saddle-bags, rifle and what remained of his grub share, then hurled it from the trail. The saddle struck the slope several yards down the steep face of the mesa, bounced, rolled and skidded until it wedged against a projecting mesquite nearly 200 feet down.

The chase party would almost certainly see it in early light, with a little luck think he'd slipped and gone over in the darkness, that the saddle had been ripped from the horse during the fall. Holding his rifle and with the saddle-bags draped around his mount's neck, Joe walked them forward. 'Watch your step, else you two will be linkin' up again,' he said, quietly.

Before first light, the trail started to level out. Joe guessed they'd soon be heading back down to the desert floor. Then there'd be stands of mesquite alongside the Gila where he'd shelter, allow his horse to recuperate. After a day or so, he'd cross the river, follow the course of the railroad east towards Phoenix and civilization.

★　★　★

Riding for a point west of the stretch of mesa, Emer looked back from a hogback ridge, made out Will in the far distance. She was surprised at first, couldn't figure out what he was doing. Then she realized he was wiping out her tracks, covering any sign that was left with his own. He was deliberately leading the pursuit away from her. She gulped with emotion and moved her mount forward to the high point of the ridge. She sky-lined herself in the hope he'd see her, raised her hand high to acknowledge what he was doing, but he gave no sign in return. She wouldn't forget Will Fawcett in a hurry. And it wasn't just because he was putting himself at risk to give her a better chance of escaping. But she wanted a singing career, and although Will's offer had been both tempting and sincere, she refused because she wasn't ready to tie herself down.

Quite a while later, and a little saddened, she turned and rode down the far side of the ridge. She'd checked her backtrail, but there'd been no sign of any posse. It appeared as though

Will's efforts to draw them off had been successful. With first dark approaching she decided to make a cold camp and rest up for the night.

Wrapped in a light blanket against the cold, Emer slept fitfully for five or six hours. Huddled on a ledge above a little arroyo she got to her feet aching and very cold. 'Singers shouldn't have to do this,' she mused, through the chatter of her teeth. Stamping her feet to get circulation going, she broke camp, saddled her mare and headed for higher country.

At the top of a long rise, she could see miles in every direction, but nothing stirred except a few, early rising scrub jays. Emer alone knew of the lawman from Yuma she'd recognized in Alto Rapino, guessed that if he'd followed them that far, he probably wouldn't be giving up just yet. And who were the others? Where were they from and who did they think they were chasing? Still, she couldn't see a puff of dust, and certainly no horsemen. She smiled stiffly, nodded east in the direction she'd last seen Will. 'Thanks. I'll remember that when you come see me,' she said quietly. 'Could be one o' them times you get lucky.'

Hipping in the saddle, she looked south across the shimmering heat-haze towards Mexico and its certain freedom. Working the lively, bustling, pioneer towns was an exciting prospect, and although peopled by men who shot and punched their way from argument and debate, they usually made for a more appreciative audience. Then she turned to the north-east, California, where she could look for and probably find work among the fast growing community settlements. She knew that beyond the Colorado Desert and the Pinto Mountains, lush new land was gradually being settled. Furthermore, it was within the compass of where Will Fawcett said he'd be taking up the plough on a homesteader's section. But Emer shouldn't and wouldn't allow that to influence her thinking. So she smiled wryly and took another lingering look to the east. Then she turned her mount and started to ride north.

★   ★   ★

After making sure at least some of the posse were following him, Will rode west for a while. At a distance, and to give the chase some bite, he traded rifle shots with three or four riders when they thought they'd pressed him into a steep-walled gully.

Although one of the pursuers would have been a scout, by riding hard, he managed to lose them in the foothills before laying a false trail north to the Gila. He made exit tracks a mile upstream, then took a chance and rode back downstream to the cover of thick stands of mesquite. When the posse reached the false trail, they rode on upstream, searching for where they thought he'd left the river.

Once they were out of sight, Will moved off again, kept downstream to where the Gila branched from the Colorado. Ten miles further north, he crossed from Arizona to the California bank, then headed west towards the land he'd heard was being offered to homesteaders.

It was risky, but he figured with a change of name and hiding behind a full beard, he should be able to claim a section and settle, make himself a home. By the time any organized law was installed and effective, he'd have a new identity, be a respectable member of the frontier community.

16

Joe Striker sat his horse in the shade of the mesquite. Wishing he had a pair of field glasses, he patiently watched for signs of movement on the far bank of the Gila.

It looked safe enough, tranquil even. All he could see was a prairie dog that seemed to be staring back at him, and a small heron. The bird took off, made a tight wheeling circle, then landed again at the water's sedge. Joe didn't know it, but he wasn't many miles from where Will had evaded the posse and headed west to the Colorado and the California border.

Joe curbed his impatience, stayed out of sight under the trees for another half-hour before making his move. Even then, he didn't immediately go into the river. He walked his rested mount back through the trees, looked up to where he'd crossed the mesa, but saw no sign of any following riders.

'I reckon I know who you guys are,' he muttered thoughtfully, made a tight, crooked smile as he turned his horse back to the bank of the Gila.

He rode out into the shallows with his carbine full-cocked and balanced on his left thigh. His eyes darted back and forth and there was a tenseness in him, an excitement now freedom was just feet away. There'd be some small town along the route of the railroad where he could get good food and a fresh horse to help him on his way.

'Yeah, reckon I could hang one or two names on you turkeys,' he said, taking a deep breath and adjusting his grip on the rifle. 'I've either thrown you, or you're here already an' lyin' in wait. Just hold off for a few minutes more,' he added hopefully.

Gradually, as he neared midstream, the river deepened. Soon his boots were trailing in the high-coloured water, then it was creeping up his legs and his horse tossed its head and started to swim. Gripping the reins and mane in his right hand, he slid into the water, held the carbine high, kicked his legs and moved close alongside his horse.

'If you're ready, now's your chance,' he mused. 'You got me like a wallowin' hog.'

And then, as if in reply to Joe's thoughts, a rifle shot cracked out. But it was from the north bank. The carbine went spinning from his grip, was claimed instantly by the muddy waters. His fingers were numbed and he made an effort to pull himself back into the saddle, but he couldn't make it.

By then he could see there were four horsemen lined up along north bank. Two of them had their rifles pointing directly at him, and he cursed his luck.

'Don't start somethin' you can't finish, Joe,' he told himself. There might or might not be anyone closing in on him along the south bank, but if he turned and tried to make it back, either side could pick him off at their leisure.

If he took flight, he'd become a duck shoot for anyone with a mind.

He had no choice but to keep moving, slanting into the shallows on the far side. By the time he made it to the bank, two of the riders were waiting, the two others kept their rifles levelled on him.

If his trigger finger hadn't been injured he might have reached for his Colt, made some sort of fight of it. But he knew that such a move would be committing suicide and he wasn't the type — well, not yet, he wasn't.

He stumbled into the shallows alongside his horse, straightened and lifted his empty hands up to shoulder level.

'That's good, Striker. Walk on out o' there,' one of the men commanded.

Joe dragged his feet through the thick cottonwood, ground his jaw in frustration because the silver badge pinned to the man's jacket carried the authority of a Territorial Arizona Ranger.

'How the hell do you know my name

. . . that I'd be crossin' here?' he demanded.

The ranger who seemed to be the leader, grinned frostily as he pushed Joe's face into the soaking shoulder of his horse, 'We know all about you, feller. We just pasted together some dodgers from your recent past. But then it only takes one feller who's holdin' a grudge to make a deal, an' we get to take advantage of it,' he said, relieving him of his Colt and clamping cuffs around his wrists.

So that was it. Joe thought he'd been betrayed. And one man who knew or could have taken a good guess at where he'd be making for was Will Fawcett. 'An' bein' paid makes you a bona fide John Judas,' he muttered under his breath.

17

The column of small wagons slowly wound its way northwest across the vast stretch of land between California's Colorado Desert and the Pinto Mountains. The train included pilgrim families who had travelled nearly 500 miles from Silver City, New Mexico. They were travelling to a 'Promised Land', or as their leader more correctly understood it to be, a government 'promise' of a 160-acre free section. They were God-fearing folk, and every night around the camp-fire, they listened to readings from the Bible, even though they were exhausted after a long day's trek. After camp had been prepared for the night, the horses had to be unharnessed and fed or hobbled on available grass. The wagons had to be checked and faults rectified, and blacksmithing meant there was little sleep for anyone. If they stopped near a good water supply, travelling barrels had to be refilled, and animals shot during the day had to be skinned and quartered.

After weeks of arduous travel, the would-be homesteaders moved in a kind of daze, numbed by the ceaseless grind of their existence. Because of their weary state, even the posted guard failed to notice the figure who staggered from the darkness one night, and into their camp ten miles east of Holland Springs.

The leader of the group having already delivered a useful chapter from 'Fences, Gates & Bridges', turned to a more spiritual and stirring passage from the Old Testament. One moment he was raising his voice with emotion, the next checking with surprise at the shadowy movement out beyond his congregation.

'Please help me. I'm alone . . . need somewhere to rest,' Emer Sparrow gasped. Her outfit was tattered, her face smeared with dust and sweat and one arm was caked with dried blood. She took a couple of steps forward, and the whole of her body trembled before she slowly collapsed.

The pilgrims' ethos of offering comfort to fellow travellers was genuine, and when Emer came around she was lying on a few rolls of blankets in back of the leader's wagon. A smiling, tired-looking woman was bent over her, work-worn fingers pressing a cool, wet flannel to her forehead.

'You're safe now, child. Whatever trouble you got ain't here, so rest easy,' she said. 'We can talk later.'

The next time Emer awoke, the wagon had stopped, the interior bright with morning sunlight. She lay quiet and thoughtful for a while, getting her bearings. Then she realized it was a man's voice, the mention of her own name, that had brought her up from sleep.

'Yeah. As I said, the tall, fair-haired one's name is Will Fawcett, an' the young redhead calls herself Emer

Sparrow,' Emer heard a low, indistinct voice saying. 'If you see either of 'em, Reverend, I'd be obliged if you'd leave word at Holland Springs. It's your next nearest town, an' we'll check when we're passin'.'

'I'll certainly do what's possible, Sheriff. You can be sure o' that,' answered a voice that Emer recognized as the man who'd been reading from the Bible when she had stumbled in to the wagon camp.

'You take good care now. Remember you ain't yet made country that's been properly tamed,' the sheriff returned.

Ten minutes later the wagons started to roll again and the man referred to as Reverend, clambered in through the flaps of the wagon's canvas canopy. He sat on the edge of a pine chest and looked down at Emer.

'Well, Miss Sparrow, it's up to you. I'll listen if you want to explain,' he said in a quiet, kindly manner.

'Thank you. I heard you, you lied for me,' she said.

The man nodded. 'Assumin' you are the woman he's seekin', I guess I was a tad lean on some o' the facts. Can't swear it would've been the same if he'd demanded a search,' he explained, looking at Emer, intently.

'Did he say what he wanted me for?' she asked.

The man nodded again. 'He says you shot his brother . . . nearly took his leg off, an' in cold blood. He says he's crippled for life.'

Emer drew in a sharp breath. 'He was Ralph Finn, the sheriff of Muletown?'

'I believe he said that was his name, yes. He, too, was carryin' a wound, but he didn't say you were the cause of it.'

'I wasn't, but I did shoot his brother. An' if it had been *cold blood*, it wouldn't have been his leg I'd shot. Do you understand what I'm sayin', Reverend?'

'I reckon I do,' he said with quiet understanding.

Emer gave a thin, tired smile and continued, 'Muletown was the Finns' town, they ran it pretty much as they liked . . . maybe still do. They put two o' my friends in jail an' I rescued 'em, because they're innocent, good men. That sheriff didn't want it that way, an' got wounded 'cause of it. We ran and later separated. One o' those friends led the pursuers away . . . gave me a chance to escape.'

'How come you walked in here lookin' like you met ol' griz?' the reverend asked.

'A big, ugly whiptail spooked my horse, an' I got thrown. That was a couple o' days ago, an' I've been watchin' your wagon train since. I was hopin' you'd stay close to the foothills, and when I saw you were goin' to stop here tonight, I started walkin'.'

'It's *two* nights, Emer. *Two* nights since you came stumblin' into camp.'

Emer blinked in surprise. 'You haven't told Finn about me?'

The reverend shook his head. 'No. I like to think I'm a fairly good judge o' character . . . reckon takin' a dislike to

165

someone like him, could save time in the long run. Besides, my good wife says trouble should be given a chair to sit in.'

'That's very broad o' you all, Reverend, an' I'm a lot more'n grateful. But I don't want to bring you any more trouble than I already have. I won't burden you for any longer than it takes me to get some of my strength back.'

'The choice is yours, Emer, but you're welcome to travel with us. We'll be passin' through several small towns before headin' out into unsettled territory, an' you can leave whenever you want. Meantime, you're our guest an' will be treated accordingly.'

Emer felt a little awkward as well as thankful. 'Thank you. Perhaps I'll sing for my supper,' she said, and smiled more openly at the reverend.

18

Indian Hat was one of a long line of small settlements that dotted the sparsely populated land of southern California. The reality as far as Will Fawcett was concerned was twofold: there was a land agency whose function it was to distribute free land for homesteading, and the nearest effective law was a hundred miles further west in San Bernadino.

Will had been long enough on the trail for his beard to make substantial growth. He told himself that if anyone was going to question a man with whiskers, they'd have full-time work for the next twenty years. His facial cover allowed him to slip into the small towns, make discreet enquiries about law officers, posses and bounty hunters within the territory.

Twenty miles north of the San

Bernardinos, he'd heard that Ralph Finn had recovered from his wound and had crossed the Colorado in search of him and Emer. He'd also heard that the man's brother, Lloyd, would remain a cripple for the rest of his life. He'd also gleaned that Joe Striker had been captured by a troop of Arizona Rangers along Arizona's stretch of the Gila River. Joe had been charged, was awaiting trial for some outlawry committed before Will had met him. There was also the matter of the attempted murder of a law officer, and that carried a much more serious charge.

Will hadn't been able to find out much about Emer, but, as luck would have it, he'd ridden from one town only an hour before the wagon train rolled in. Emer was almost unrecognizable with her hair cut short and wearing a hopsack dress. She worked alongside the other pilgrims at their chores, even sat with them at their readings around the camp-fire at night. It was a perfect cover for her as she moved further up country.

⋆ ⋆ ⋆

Will was unaware of this, as he, too, continued his journey. In due course, he eventually reached Mallard Wells and sought out John Erwitt who was one of California's land agents. But when he enquired about free homestead land, Erwitt sucked air between his pursed lips, slowly shook his head.

'I'm afraid you've arrived a bit late, Mr Johnson,' he said. 'All the settlement tracts are gone.'

'All of it?' Will asked incredulously.

'Yeah, just about. There is a full section left out at Blackbone Flag, but there's several parties after it. I figured the only reasonable way's to run a ballot.'

Will looked interested. 'You mean, put all the names into a hat and draw one out?'

'Yeah, the luck o' the draw,' Erwitt

169

agreed. 'It'll be run properly with a scrutinizer, o' course. Like I say, quite a few folk are already after that last section. They know that when it's gone, it'll be some time before more land's thrown open. You can always stake yourself a claim up near the Deadman Lakes. There's drawbacks there, though . . . hard, bad men of every feather. An' there's talk o' runnin' a railroad spur up from Pasadena to Barstow. You wouldn't get much if they wanted you out for right of way.'

Will nodded. 'I'm not real certain what you're tryin' to say,' he said distractedly, 'but perhaps you can tell me how to find this Blackbone Flag.'

Erwitt adjusted his spectacles, rubbed the bridge of his nose. 'Yeah, 'course I can. I'll even give you a map. But what's the point after what I've just told you?' he said, looking slightly perturbed.

'Well, that's my problem. Me an' them others in the ballot,' Will said. 'It ain't closed, is it?'

'No. There's another two days.'

Will gave a tolerant smile. 'Plenty o' time to look the section over then. If I decide I like the look of it, I'll pop my name into the box. Unless you know o' some reason why I shouldn't?' he added tentatively.

'No, no reason, it's open to all,' the agent replied stiffly. 'It's just that local folk might not like it if a stranger rode in an' got lucky.'

'That's what ballots are usually about, Mr Erwitt. Gettin' lucky,' Will answered back. 'You're beginnin' to make it sound as if chance don't extend to strangers,' he added with a severe look.

Erwitt coloured, moved uncomfortably in his chair. 'I just told you it would be run properly.'

'Good. Now if you'd let me have that map you mentioned,' Will said.

As soon as Will had cleared town, Erwitt started huffing and puffing. Looking worried, he pulled on his derby, locked his office and hurried down the street to one of Indian Hat's two saloons.

171

Once through the batwings of the lively Desert Rose, Erwitt went straight to the curtained doorway that lead to a private room. A big, deceptively sleepy-looking guard didn't bother unfolding his arms when the land agent approached, merely lifted insensible eyes under the brim of his range hat.

'I've got to see Mr Kewell,' Erwitt said anxiously.

'Well, he's busy, so you can't. Come back later,' he growled rudely.

'It's about Blackbone Flag.' Erwitt's voice had a nervy edge. 'If he finds out you stopped me tellin him', you won't be comin' back at all.'

The man named Max Shume, frowned. He was coarse featured and towered above Erwitt, was hired for his appearance more than his wits. 'If I'm not back in one minute, come through,' he said abruptly and turned through the beaded curtain.

Erwitt stepped into a large office where a man of middle years was buttoning his vest in front of a standing mirror. He was bald and clean shaven, had pale eyes and a scar that warped his upper lip. As though with a permanent scowl, he watched Erwitt's reflection.

'What's this about Blackbone Flag?' he said curtly.

The agent removed his derby, held it between his nervous fingers. 'A stranger just rode in . . . came to see me about homesteadin' land.'

'Yeah? An' you told him there ain't any. If he's a stranger, how'd the Flag section come up?' Lester Kewell asked with quiet menace. He walked to a deeply upholstered chair and dropped into it, drummed the fingers of both hands on the top of his desk.

'I told him there was only Blackbone Flag left. That it was goin' to be decided by ballot within a couple o' days. He could make trouble if he finds out I kept it from him.'

After a while, Kewell nodded. 'He should be satisfied then. Is that all you're here tellin' me?'

'No. He's asked directions out there. He wants to take a look . . . says if he likes it, he'll put his name into the ballot.'

Kewell's eyes bored enquiringly at the land agent. 'So there's another name to deal with. I thought you were takin' care of all that. I still don't know what it is you're botherin' me with.'

'I got a feelin' this feller ain't goin' to be content with puttin' his name on a piece o' paper to drop in a makeshift ballot box. I thought it best you know that.'

'Did he give you a name?'

'Johnson. He looks to me like someone who, once he's got his mind set, don't give in. Like him,' Erwitt added with a glance towards Shume. 'But there's another side, somethin' underlyin'. Believe me, he's trouble waitin'.'

Kewell cracked his knuckles as he leaned forward, closer to Erwitt. 'How can he make trouble for us? Why should he? Nothin's changed.' Kewell grunted as an encouragement for Erwitt to see his point of view. 'There's plenty of others who've put their mark down for that ballot. Get the storekeeper's wife to make the draw . . . anybody's wife. Just make sure it's Shume's name they take out. All you got to do then is destroy anythin' that needs destroyin'. You understand that?'

Erwitt looked miserable but nodded his agreement. 'Yeah, I've always understood, Mr Kewell,' he muttered. 'I came to tell you my misgivin's that's all. I'll handle things the way you want, like I always do. Remember, you'll have to prove-up on that land within the time limit. There's nothin' I can do to get around that.'

'Get the plot registered. I'll worry about the other stuff,' Kewell said sharply. Then he beckoned for Shume to escort the land agent from the room.

'Do you want me to discourage this Johnson feller, boss?' Shume asked, a minute or so later.

'Maybe. Let's see how far his interest stretches,' Kewell replied.

19

Blackbone Flag was exactly the kind of spot Will had been looking for. There was permanent water from a fast-flowing creek, lush grass and stands of good cedar for building. It was a long way from town, beyond all the other land that had been homesteaded, and the Cottonwood Hills were only a few miles further to the west.

As he rode the boundary of the section, Will studied the map that Erwitt had given him. The land was more than he'd ever hoped for. Before he was done, he had envisaged a site for the cabin, considered its outlook, even paced out its foundation. Halfway up the rising slope of a natural bench with a summer pasture behind him, he could command a fine view in all directions — more than 600 acres of prime, cattle-rearing land.

A couple of miles back in the direction of town, Will stopped off and introduced himself to Blackbone Flag's nearest homesteader. Saul Blocker and his wife had three young kids, and although they all looked weathered and worn, they appeared content if not happy.

'Gives a man fulfilment workin' for hisself, Mr Johnson,' Blocker was saying to Will, over a cup of coffee. 'Yessir, a whole heap o' fulfilment.'

'How come that Blackbone Flag wasn't snapped up before?' Will asked.

Blocker shrugged. 'Too far out for most folk. Us with wives an' kids need to be nearer town for supplies . . . schoolin' an the like. I'd have liked it myself, but couldn't work that much land. A quarter section's about all I can handle. Besides, Kewell was after it about the same time, an' I didn't come out here lookin' for trouble.'

A look of concern suddenly tightened Mrs Blocker's features and Will frowned.

'What trouble?' he asked.

'Saul, you be careful with your tongue,' the woman advised her husband who held up his hand to placate her.

'Mr Johnson has a right to know what he's up against if he's goin' to file a claim on Blackbone Flag,' he answered back.

'Yeah, I aim to put my name in the ballot,' Will said. 'I've taken a long ride around an' I reckon I can handle the work, if that's what you mean.'

'No it weren't that,' Blocker said, looking uncertain. 'I was meanin' you'll be up against a rigged ballot. O' course if you've just hit town, you won't know that. But mark my words, Mr Johnson, that land's already got a name stamped on it.'

'Whose name?' Will asked more brusquely than he meant.

'Lester Kewell. He owns the saloon, as well as half the town an' a big spread beyond the Cottonwoods. Now he wants to grab half the open range.'

'So why does he want Blackbone Flag?'

'At the moment he drives his herds down the range to pick up the trailherds headin' for Nevada. If he had to bring 'em *around* the Cottonwoods, he'd have another hundred miles or more. He wants the Flag section so's he can drive through without havin' to do that, and at any time he likes.'

'What about other folk who were interested?'

'A couple of 'em were visited by Max Shume — that's Kewell's pet thug. After a short talk with *him*, they decided to resettle up near the China Lakes. So now Blackbone Flag's the only piece o' land left. The only way Kewell can make sure o' keepin' the trail open is to get it in his own name.'

Will studied Blocker while he turned a thought over. 'I thought homestead land was for folk who don't have any o' their own,' he said a moment later. 'Surely that measure don't fit in with this Kewell feller?'

Blocker smiled crookedly. 'That's why it'll be in Shume's name. Kewell will give him all the men he needs to prove-up by deadline, then Shume'll sell back to him. It ain't much of a secret in these parts.'

'That's right enough,' the man's wife said nervously. 'But the sensible ones don't blather about it.'

'This ain't blather, Ellie. An' you know better than for us to let Mr Johnson walk into it unaware.'

'Yeah, I know it,' the woman sighed her agreement. Then she looked swiftly at Will. 'But please don't mention it was Saul . . . us, who told you,' she appealed.

'Told me *what?*' Will said with a positive smile.

★   ★   ★

Shortly afterwards and in pensive mood, Will rode back to Indian Hat. As soon as he arrived he called in to the land agent's office, told Erwitt to add his name to the ballot.

'If my name don't come out o' that

box, I'll be askin' someone to take out the remainin' papers an' open 'em up. If I don't find my name in there, I'll put a bullet in your wretched hide,' Will threatened.

Erwitt was immediately shaken, too alarmed to say anything in response and Will knew then that Saul Blocker was right. Only moments after Will left the office, the agent once again hurried to Lester Kewell's saloon.

Will ordered a whiskey and beer chaser, was halfway through the beer when, in the back-bar mirror, he saw a big man come up behind him, close enough to give him a dig in the side and gruff out a few words.

Will turned slowly, took a long, hard stare at where the man had prodded him. 'There's room enough here, feller, so I'm hopin' that was some sort o' clumsy blunder,' he said evenly.

'It was to help you pay for them drinks.'

Will narrowed his eyes. 'I already have. If it's anythin' to do with you.'

Shume shook his head. 'I ain't seen any money cross the counter. These drinks ain't paid for, are they?' he called to the nearest bartender.

Without a change of sour expression, the bartender shook his head. 'No, not yet.'

'How many times I told you not to serve any o' these goddamn saddle-bums without seein' the colour o' their money? They pay for each an' every drink they take.'

The bartender was already turning away. 'Sorry, Shume, I forgot,' he muttered and Will realized it was a well-worked, almost tiresome routine.

Shume reached out to grab his arm and Will cursed, tossed the remains of his beer up into the man's face.

'Whoops, that's a goddamn saddle-bum's way o' tellin' you the drinks are paid for,' he muttered daringly.

Immediately, the general clamour of the saloon ceased, and Shume wiped his dripping face on his sleeve, bared his teeth in a malicious grin. 'I was kind o' hopin' you'd do somethin' like that,' he rasped.

'Yeah, I thought so,' Will returned. 'You're about as hard to read as a kids' learner. But I ain't, an' if it's trouble you want,' he added, as he smashed the empty beer glass into the middle of the man's face, 'I'll goddamn oblige you.'

There was a gasp from the crowd as Shume staggered back. His arms were flailing and his face was a mask of fresh, running blood. Grabbing the edge of the bar he steadied himself, shook his head, then charged at Will with clenched fists.

Will stood his ground and, as the big man drew close, he suddenly lifted his right leg and drove his boot into Shume's ample stomach. The man's impetus added to the force of the kick, and Will took a step back. But Shume doubled over as the breath gusted from him, and Will went forward, brought his knee up savagely into the man's bloodied face.

There was a dull crunch, and Shume

went down to his knees, head hanging and blood dripping into the sawdusted floor. Will drew his Colt and whipped the barrel across the side of the fallen man's head. Then he swung around and triggered off a single shot at the figure he'd noticed standing at the top of the staircase.

The bullet from Will's Colt crashed into the ceiling above the lone gunman. He took a sideways step, stumbled and clattered down the stairs to sprawl in a heap at the bottom. Men emerged from where they'd dived for cover, stared at Will, then the unconscious Shume, then to the man lying dead with a broken neck.

Lester Kewell stood pale and tight-lipped. He was holding back one side of the beaded curtains with the shaking land agent close behind him. He levelled his gaze on Will who, still holding the smoking Colt, stared back at him edgily.

'Are you Kewell? Lester Kewell?' he asked.

The saloon owner returned a short nod of agreement. 'An' who the hell are you?' he followed up with.

'Will Johnson. An' I'm here to see there's a fair ballot for the section o' homesteadin' land known as Blackbone Flag. I've already told the agent that as soon as the ballot's drawn, I want a look at the papers. I'll be expectin' to see the names of every man an' woman who's put in for that land.' Will waited, but Kewell didn't make a move and said nothing. 'If it don't look proper, what's just happened here will be me just horsin' around,' he concluded.

Will gave Kewell another hard look and, still holding his Colt, thumbed the hammer and backed out through the batwings.

20

There were four prisoners in the tumbleweed wagon. They were drawn up behind the boarded-up store that was being used by the Arizona Rangers as temporary headquarters in the small township of Caliente. Like the other three men, Joe Striker had his wrists and ankles shackled. He sat with his back against the mesh cage.

The rangers had collected the last fugitive they'd been searching for that very afternoon. Soon the wagon would be hitched to a team of mules, and they'd start on the gruelling leg of the journey to the Territorial Prison at Yuma. At best, Joe could hope for a few years breaking rocks along the banks of the Colorado River, at worst it would be a summary conviction and the hangman's rope.

As it turned out, Joe spent two weeks

in a gloomy cell, while waiting trial. But it was long enough for him to decide he didn't want brutal control and restricting walls, no matter how long or short the sentence. So when the judge ruled five years on the rockpile, he figured to do something about it. He knew the only chance left to make an escape was when they were being transferred from the cells of the Yuma Court House, back to the prison.

His fellow passengers were those who'd ridden with him from Caliente. One of them — a Mexican killer who was due to hang the next day — had previously thrown some sort of fit that had scared the hell out of Joe and the others. They were close enough to know it wasn't just a bout of terror sickness. Nevertheless, when the full impact of the man's sentence hit home, Joe was sure something similar would happen again. And now the man was showing the signs again; fast, shallow breaths, trembling limbs and flecks of foam at the corners of his mouth. When he knocked the offered dipper of water from Joe's hand, Joe knew it created a chance to escape.

The other two prisoners had flinched away. 'Stay away from him. He's got the goddamn rabies,' one of them stuttered out fearfully.

'Guard,' Joe yelled. 'This goddamn chilli-eater's gone crazy. He'll kill us all if he bites us. Get down here.'

In fact, the Mexican was having a seizure and rapidly approaching a state of unconsciousness. The violent contracting of his muscles caused his body to jerk around wildly and it did look as though he was trying to attack or bite one of his criminal companions.

Moments after Joe's distress call, the armed guard jumped down from where he'd been seated alongside the wagon's driver.

But Joe was ready. He twisted down to the bed of the vehicle and wedged himself half under the Mexican. He let out a tormented howl as he played the injured party, as he eyed the guard fumbling with the padlock. As the guard pulled at the door and dragged it open, the driver arrived and together they reached in to drag the Mexican off Joe.

Seizing the moment, Joe lashed out with his manacled feet. He caught the guard savagely across the point of his jaw, and the man went down instantly unconscious. The driver backed away reaching for his Colt, but Joe launched himself up and forward. He went to ground with the man, slammed an iron bound wrist at his head as they hit the dirt.

Joe was suddenly in a desperate situation, knew there'd be an unimaginable legal reckoning unless he got away. He struck the driver again, then again until he lay there groaning, pleading for someone to help him. He searched the man's pockets but one of the other prisoners yelled out that it was the guard who had the keys. A moment later, Joe had freed himself from his leg irons, handed the keys over to have his cuffs unlocked. Within minutes, all four of them were unfettered, and the befuddled Mexican killer was sitting up wondering what had happened.

'I'm obliged, feller. Don't know what it is ails you, but it's sure opportune.' Joe said, as he took the driver's Colt and stuffed it through his pants belt. Then he unharnessed the lead mule, picked up the guard's carbine and mounted the animal bareback. His three companions would spend a few minutes making up their minds, then make their way south and get lost in the San Louis Mesa. But Joe was heading north-west up into California.

'There's someone I got to pick a bone with,' he told them with a humourless grin.

21

As Lester Kewell walked into the crowded land agency office, he smirked at the way a few folk stood aside to let him through. He was accompanied by Max Shume and another accomplice named Newton Brass. There were a few chairs set about, and John Erwitt smiled nervously as he gestured for the men to take them.

From where he'd set up the ballot box behind his desk, Erwitt looked uneasily at the few folk who had turned up for the draw. Most were actual ballotees, a few were just interested. His heart thumped a little more when he saw Will Fawcett come in quietly and stand to one side of the doorway.

'Well, folks,' Erwitt began after a noisy clearing of his throat. 'This is the first land ballot we've ever had in Indian Hat. There's word in from

Bakersfield that head office is mighty pleased with the way folk out here have proved-up on other homestead land . . . the way they've stuck to the deadlines. There's only one or two ain't made it, but *they* got caught up in special circumstances.'

'Well, we *did* make it, so get a move on,' Shume growled, when he got a nudge from Kewell. Will noticed Shume's face was looking raw, guessed the man's head bones were still paining him from when he'd cracked him with his Colt.

Erwitt, who looked as though he'd settle for postponing the draw indefinitely, cleared his throat again. 'Yeah, I guess you folk are kind of eager to get the results,' he said, forcing a tense grin and with a swift glance in Will's direction. 'I've asked Mrs Hegarty to make the actual draw. Is that OK with everyone?'

'We don't care if it's a pig that sticks its goddamn tail in. Just do it,' Shume called out impatiently, again.

The others were also keen to get the ballot over with, and without further ado, Erwitt invited a woman of straight-laced appearance, up to the desk to make the draw.

The land agent opened the padlock and flipped back the small trapdoor lid. 'If you don't mind, Mrs Hegarty, just reach in an' take out one slip. That'll be the winner, an' I wish everyone the best of luck,' he added unconvincingly.

'Just pick out a goddamn name,' Kewell said himself this time.

The general store-keeper's wife threw him a frosty look, eased back a cuff of her blouse and reached into the box. After stirring her hand around for a second or two, like she was hanging trout, she withdrew a folded slip of paper. She smoothed it out between her forefinger and thumb, held it at arm's length and squinted. 'The winner is . . . William Johnson,' she said in her slightly cracked voice.

A lot of the colour drained from Land Agent Erwitt's face, and in a moment there was a palpable sense of discontent within the room. Baffled disbelief, then anger distorted Lester Kewell's features.

'William Johnson?' he shouted, as he leapt to his feet. 'A stranger who rides into town suddenly wins Blackbone Flag? Someone's been messin' with that goddamn box.'

Looking appropriately bewildered, Will acknowledged the cool looks, then the grudging best wishes from a couple of townsfolk as he walked to the front. He stepped up beside Erwitt who visibly flinched, looked around the room challengingly as Mrs Hegarty returned to her seat.

'Folks, Mr Kewell's right. The ballot box *was* messed about with. By *me*.' He held up his hands swiftly at the gasps and sudden outbreak of murmuring. 'I did it last night ... well, early this mornin'. It weren't exactly heavily guarded. I mean, who would have expected someone to attempt such a thing?' he added with blatant cynicism.

Shume and Brass both stood to side with their boss as the man continued angrily, 'Goddamn polecat's made fools of us all,' he shouted.

Will faced him squarely and waited for the clamour to subside. Then he reached into his shirt pocket and drew out a small bundle of carefully folded papers. 'These are the paper slips I took out o' the box,' he said, holding them up. 'Here, Erwitt, hand 'em round. Everyone take a good look at the name on 'em.'

While the trembling agent handed out the ballot slips, Will continued, 'By checkin' a bit, I found out who was interested in the land . . . who'd put in for the ballot. Well, for one reason or another, there was fewer than you'd think . . . five. If you want to know why, take a ride up to the China Lakes an' ask the families who've recently settled there.' Will looked hard at Max Shume before he went on, 'Anyway, I wrote the names o' them who'd balloted . . . them who thought they'd balloted, on new bits o' paper and put them back in the box where they should've been. You've just seen the good lady here draw *my* name out, an' I can tell you it's the only slice o' luck I've had in nigh on ten years. That's somethin I won't be apologizin' for.'

'The name on this paper says Shume,' someone called out.

'That's what I've been tellin' you,' Will replied. 'The papers I took out, have all got his name on 'em.'

'That's right. It's here too ... Shume.'

'An' on this one.'

'It's his name written on all of 'em,' a fourth man yelled.

'Yeah. But what we got to ask ourselves, is it really the big ugly monkey's work, or is it the grinder who he's workin' for?'

Mrs Hegarty gasped with shock, ushered the womenfolk from the office. The men who now remained were the wronged ballotees, and they bravely faced up to Kewell and his two menacing henchmen.

'He's lyin',' the saloon owner told them. 'Goddamn blow-in's stolen our land an' he's bluffin' his way out.'

Will shook his head forlornly. 'They know what happened, Kewell. They even know *how* an' *who*. They just needed someone to show 'em. You'll find all their names are there, includin' yours. It's been a fair draw, despite you an' your gorillas. The same goes for the land agent, himself.'

'They said they'd float me to the Gulf if I didn't go along with 'em.' Erwitt blustered fearfully.

'Keep your mouth shut,' Kewell yelled. The man was breathing heavy as he kept his eyes on Will. Then he stepped to one side, nodded at Shume and Brass.

Men dived for the floor, scuttled for cover as the two hired guns reached for their Colts. But Will had the advantage, was already bringing up his own Colt as he dropped to one knee beside Erwitt's desk. His first shot took Brass in the side, making the man turn and stagger before collapsing in a heap. Shume made a fast shot, but his bullet thudded low into the front of the desk.

Now, with a steady two-handed grip, Will fired again. Shume wasn't fast enough to move and got hit in the chest. He lifted to his toes, attempted to raise his gun hand but fell back against the wall. He turned his head as if looking for Brass, then he dropped his Colt, his legs buckled slowly and he slid insensibly to the floor.

'They made the first move,' Will rasped. 'There's enough o' you saw it.'

Lester Kewell who had his gun half drawn, stared in disbelief at Shume's body, recoiled as the toe of Brass's boot jerked in pain-filled anguish. Then he saw Will's Colt swing in his direction and he let go of his gun and stretched out his hands.

'Don't shoot,' he croaked, with a shake of his head, raising his hands higher.

'Shootin's all finished, Kewell,' Will

replied, as he walked over to face the shaky saloon owner. 'An' *you* lost. Stupid thing is, you stood as much chance as anyone o' gettin' your name pulled out o' that box.'

'But I ain't a gunfighter,' he breathed out hoarsely.

'No, an' *them* you paid to be, weren't up to much either.' Will rammed the muzzle of his gun hard into the man's stomach. Kewell gagged, doubled up as his muscles and nerve gave out. Will leaned over him, gave him a sharp kick. 'An' don't pay anyone else to come after me. If you do, I'll return 'em on a wagon when I come lookin' for you.'

Will holstered his Colt and turned to the few people who were left shuffling about anxiously. 'I never wanted trouble,' he said. 'All I want now, is to be left alone to prove-up on Blackbone Flag. An' in case any o' you are worried about a right o' way, there'll always be an open an' free one . . . just thought you should know.' Then he looked at Erwitt. 'When you've got this place cleaned up, we'll see about registerin' that land.'

'Yessir, Mr Johnson,' the land agent replied hurriedly, wiping his face with a big kerchief. 'We don't want any more trouble.'

22

Joe Striker had watched the dust cloud for a long time. Staying low, he'd hurried to get ahead of the rider, whoever it might be. Two hours before that, he'd turned his mule loose. The animal was only a harness broke and didn't take to being ridden bareback. Since then he'd walked nearly ten miles on foot and badly needed a saddle horse.

Following the course of a narrow arroyo, the man rode close. He wasn't particularly watchful, and when Joe sprang out from where he'd been crouched below the rift in the arid scrubland, the man simply let out a yell of alarm. Joe ran a few steps, leaped up, took a strong seize and they both fell back. The man hit the ground heavily and Joe twisted to land way from him. The man made a winded gasp and Joe stumbled to his feet, pulled the Colt he'd taken from the prison wagon guard.

While the man was still dazed, Joe relieved him of his old Walker, rammed it into his own gunbelt and nudged the man with the toe of his boot.

The man coughed and shook his head as he sat up.

'Well, you could've shot me, so by the looks o' you, I'm hopin' it's my horse you're wantin',' he suggested, after he'd regained a breath.

'Yeah, that's right, feller, an' I'm real sorry. You're goin' to have to loan me your boots too. Mine are just about all in.'

The man looked up, squinted for a moment, then pulled off his boots and tossed them towards Joe. 'You from Bakersfield?' he asked, making out Joe's prison outfit.

'Yuma,' Joe corrected. 'How far are we from a town . . . a ranch?'

'A long way. We're miles from anywhere.'

'You know these parts?'

'Yeah, some,' the man said. 'I work for a San Diego stock buyer. I ride until I find a likely herd . . . take a percentage if there's a sale. It ain't too lucrative, but I get to meet a whole lot o' fascinatin' characters,' he added drily.

'Would one of 'em go by the name o' Fawcett . . . Johnson, maybe?' Joe asked. 'He'd be new to these parts. But the last time I heard, he was taken' up one o' them free homesucker sections.'

The cattle negotiator was already shaking his head slowly. 'There ain't much left down here other than north o' the San Bernardinos. I did hear there was some trouble over a land parcel . . .'

'That'll be him,' Joe interrupted eagerly. 'Where'd this happen?'

'Indian Hat, I think. But I don't know about anyone named Johnson.'

'Oh it's *him* all right,' Joe said. 'Did you hear anythin' else?'

'Big augur . . . name o' Kewell, was involved. He uses his own crew to drive herds up to the Nevada border. I remember, 'cause he sounds like someone I should go see.'

'Yeah, why not?' Joe muttered thoughtfully. 'How do I get to this Indian Hat?'

When Joe had directions, he told the man to find some shade. 'Rest up till the heat o' the day goes. An' bear in mind I got a memory for faces.' he warned, as he drew the man's gun and tossed it away.

'Yeah, so have I. Yours makes mine the easier job,' the man said unsmiling, glaring at Joe's unprepossessing features. 'An' there ain't any goddamn shade.'

★ ★ ★

At first dark, the man started his walk in Joe's worn boots. They hurt his feet almost immediately but he had little choice, moved off in the direction of the town he'd been heading for earlier in the day.

The following morning he was

staggering with fatigue when, through the shimmer of rising heat, he made out a horseman running down from a distant ridge. The man rode with his rifle angled into the sky, its butt braced against his thigh. As he drew close he reined down, turned his horse until he was sideways to the still rising sun.

'Hell, I was hopin' you was someone else,' the man said. He pushed the rifle into its saddle scabbard, then flipped back his jacket to reveal an Arizona Rangers shield. 'Name's Leo Tuckwell, an' I'm lookin' for an escaped prisoner. Maybe you can help,' he stated.

The cattle agent kneeled in weariness, nodded as he reached up for the canteen the ranger offered him. 'Reckon I can,' he croaked, before taking a long pull of tepid water. 'Can even let you have his boots in support.'

23

Ralph Finn was no longer carrying out his duties as the sheriff of Muletown. He'd been too long away, hadn't appointed any deputies, and the citizens were left to get along as best they could.

His brother Lloyd still didn't get around too well. According to an expensive Lake Mead doctor, his right kneecap was a splintered mess and beyond healing. When he got to walking again, it would be painful, and with the aid of a crutch or stick, at best.

The songbird would pay for what she'd done. It cut into Ralph Finn, ran two-up with his loathing for Joe Striker. Striker had humiliated and goaded him on his own patch, and from the pistol-whipping he'd received, head-aches were a regular and debilitating occurrence. No one was going to inflict that upon him and get away with it. As for Will Fawcett, well, he'd pay the price of being their partner. Through the bars of his jailhouse cell, Finn had threatened to chase them all down and exact his vengeance. And within his own credo, he was a man of his word.

He and Lloyd had had a good thing going in Muletown. They'd got the place sewn up, ran it pretty much as they liked and raked in plenty of dollars. Now it all had to be given up because of Striker, Fawcett, and Emer Sparrow.

Wherever he went, Ralph Finn still claimed to be sheriff of Muletown, or Mule County as he'd now got to call it. He used the badge and an overblown authority to get information and food and lodging, even ammunition when he was low on funds. He'd wired Lloyd on a few occasions for more money, but because of desolate terrain and remoteness he didn't know how long his brother could manage to keep forwarding it.

Now he was low on cash again, and

his horse badly needed shoeing. More problematic was the fact that in southern California there was more resistance to his 'lawman's right' than there'd been in his Muletown territory. In one border town he was told his jurisdiction was doubtful, so when he rode his limping mount into Blue Sky, he wondered if he was going to get any co-operation by presenting his badge of office.

He dismounted outside the saloon, turned his lame horse into the hitch rail and loosely tied the reins. He didn't have nearly enough cash for a new mount, so he thought he'd try his alternative influence with the livery-man. But wanting to get a measure of the town first, he went into the saloon and ordered a dust-cutter whiskey. He downed it at a single gulp, and ordered another.

Both times the bartender made no attempt to pour the drinks until Finn snapped his money on the counter.

He sighed, recognizing procedure for

drifters and chancers.

After a minute or two and a covert look around him, his interest was aroused by one particular dust-caked, dishevelled customer. The man was talking to a small group of drinkers who were gathered at the far end of the bar. In between taking long pulls of his beer, he was relating what sounded like a fascinating story.

'An' if that ranger hadn't happened along, I'd have ridden the long trail all right. Even he was ready to plug me on sight,' he said, shooting an exaggerated line.

'Ha, who'd he think you were, Mad Dog Kelly?' one of the men chortled, pushing another beer forward.

'Could've been. He was on the run from Yuma Pen . . . told me hisself.'

Finn cursed, walked quickly over to the group who were pressing the man for more information. 'Did you say this feller was out o' Yuma? Was he called Striker?' he demanded. 'The ranger must've told you his name.'

'Yeah, that's what he called him . . . Striker. That an' a few other cuss words.'

Finn grinned coldly. 'I didn't get all o' your story, friend,' he said. 'How about you tell it to me from the beginnin'?'

'Then I'll be needin' a little more juice, *friend*,' the man returned. 'I ain't goin' through this again for nothin'.'

Finn called the bartender over. 'More whiskey an' another beer for him,' he ordered impatiently.

When the drinks came, the man took another thirsty gulp, licked his lips and smirked self-importantly before repeating the bit about how he'd had his horse stolen by Joe Striker. He looked down, indicated the shabby prison boots. 'Them's what he left me with.' Then he took a sudden, sharp look at Finn. 'Are you some sort o' reporter?' he asked.

Finn shook his head disinterestedly. 'Where's this ranger? Is he still around?'

'No, he ain't. He took off for Indian

210

Hat . . . wanted to send a wire an' get himself a fresh horse. It was where Striker was headed to find this partner o' his.'

'Did Striker mention who he was . . . who he was lookin' for?'

'Yeah. It was me said I'd heard o' him. His name was Johnson. Will Johnson.'

While he thought, Finn stared impassively at the empty glasses on the bar top. He'd already picked up that Will Fawcett was using another name. Now it looked as though he was closing in on his quarry. If only he could get to Indian Hat, ahead of the ranger. He knew of a man in Indian Hat, too. He was a businessman, a long-arm associate of Lloyd's. He'd be of doubtful standing or integrity, but nevertheless, a contact.

'You're talkin' to Sheriff Ralph Finn out o' Mule County, Arizona,' he claimed, showing his silver star to the men around him. 'I'm after this man Striker, an' need to get to him before that ranger does. I need a good, fast horse, an' I've got the authority to seize one unless someone loans me one.'

When there was no fitting offer, he put his badge back in his shirt pocket. He had a short attempt to stare the customers down, then strode across the room and out through the batwings. Standing on the boardwalk, he looked at the line of horses that were tethered at the hitch rail, took a moment to settle on a long-legged roan. As he stepped down into the street to unhitch the reins, a man pushed out through the batwings.

'Hey, get the hell away from my horse,' he shouted, bunching his fists in anger. 'You ain't takin' my property, goddamn lawman or not.'

'Sorry, friend, I need it. You'll get it back,' Finn retaliated.

'I said, you ain't takin' it.'

As Finn swung into the saddle, the man cursed, reached for his revolver as he jumped down the steps.

But the lawman's body was shielding

his right hand. He pulled his own Colt, leaned down and cracked the barrel sharply across the top of the man's head. 'Observe an' obey the word o' the law,' he rasped and jammed his spurs hard and high behind his horse's ribs.

24

Will Johnson, formerly Fawcett, dropped the head of his big, woodsman's axe to the ground. He took a couple of steps back as the cedar wavered, made crackling splintering sounds as it started to fall. It came down with an almighty crash and the air was filled with swirling leaves and the sounds of startled birds and critters. Then the crushing silence of the woods returned, settled close around him once again.

He wiped his face with a sweat-grimed bandanna and his torso glistened. This was the tenth cedar he'd felled, and he figured it was time to start trimming and splitting, sawing and making notches. But first he needed a rest.

Taking his canteen from a low-hanging branch, he walked over to a cedar he'd felled earlier and sat on the end of the trunk. He drank deeply, poured a little over his head and neck, and gave a tired smile. Then he built a cigarette.

He didn't normally take tobacco, but someone told him the smoke helped to keep midges and mites away. He looked around the area he'd cleared and levelled for the site of his cabin, where he'd lay the sills. It would start as a single room, but later he'd divide and extend it with a kitchen and parlour, maybe a bedroom. It wasn't ever going to be anything elaborate, but he *was* going to build a significant fireplace. He knew on occasion there'd be bitterly cold winds that swept across the land, and he didn't aim to sit inside and shiver because of it. He'd already carried a couple hundred stones up from the creek bottoms and piled them at one end of the levelled plot. Then there'd be a sign to cut and whittle a droll plaque that said: 'At home everything is easy'.

He knew he'd have to be careful with his finances next time he was in

Indian Hat. He had to maintain a stash for essentials like nails and coffee, not be tempted by fumadiddles and tinned luxuries. He could more or less feed himself by shooting rabbits and prairie chickens and catching fish from the creek, even though it meant time away from building and clearing more land.

As for Lester Kewell, Will was aware that the man had been conspicuous by his absence, but in the last few days, he'd seen a couple of riders watching him. Unmoving, they'd sat their horses atop the ridge that overlooked his intended home pasture. When he'd ridden up there and followed their tracks, they'd led off towards the Cottonwoods — the direction of the Kewell spread.

Will had already figured the men were line riders taking back news of his progress. Kewell would be biding his time, waiting until the cabin was finished and some fences erected before he made any sort of move. 'Huh, sure got the makins' of a fine line-shack,'

Will had muttered wryly. Well it would either be that, or he'd destroy all of the work, make sure Will didn't prove-up by the deadline. As it stood, a full section was a lot of range for one man to watch over while trying to work it at the same time.

Will shrugged. He knew the skirmish with Kewell and his henchmen was nothing more than a flex for what was coming later. Kewell had grumbled into his lair, and when he was hungry enough, he'd emerge dangerous.

All of a sudden, Will snuffed the tip of his cigarette, reached out for his rifle that was propped against the cedar's stump. He dropped to one knee and levered a shell into the breech, then lifted the weapon to his shoulder. He aimed in the direction of the trees where he'd heard the low, soft whinny of an approaching horse. Now from close by, his own loose-tethered mount pricked up its ears, stamped its forefoot and snorted a reply.

Will let the rifle barrel drop as he

slowly got to his feet, mouthed a few words as the rider came from cover.

'I was wonderin' if that invitation still stands?' The girl gave an open smile and folded her hands on the saddle horn. 'You know, the invitation to a songbird named Sparrow to look up a bearded feller named Johnson?' Then she took off her hat to reveal her severely cut red hair.

Will was taken completely by surprise. 'Hello, Emer. Sorry, it weren't *you* I was expectin',' he faltered. As he stepped forward to help her dismount, he discreetly let the rifle fall to the ground behind him. 'I ain't got a decent chair for you to sit yourself in. Huh, I ain't got *any* sort o' chair, yet. But if you'd like to take this spot, it'll give you an idea,' he said.

Emer seated herself on the trunk of the felled cedar. 'Beats another few hours on a ten-dollar saddle.'

Still taken aback, Will shook his head, continued to stare at her. 'The only jawbone I get's usually with somethin' on four legs,' he offered uncomfortably. 'It's been a long time.'

'It hasn't been *that* long, Will.'

'It is when you ain't prepared,' Will responded quickly. 'I meant what I said then, Emer. I guess I ain't changed that much.'

Emer nodded agreeably. 'Whatever it was I wanted, I either got it, or it weren't there. So here I am then. A sort o' bad penny.'

Then, knowing she had to satisfy some of his curiosity, she told him about being picked up by the pilgrims from Silver City. 'They were mighty good to me, Will, but I weren't their kind o' folk. They were goin' to give me everythin' an' I was goin' to take it before lettin' 'em down. They had Bible readin's two times a day — three on Sunday, for Chris'sakes.' Emer waited until Will smiled before she went on. 'To save awkward feelin's all round, I just slipped away one night.'

'Where'd you end up? California ain't one big squatters' mission,' Will said.

'Indian Hat. I thought there might be work. It's what I said I'd do, remember?'

Will nodded, said he did. 'So what happened?'

'Nothin' much. Everyone was talkin' about a man named William Johnson who took on the territory's big bull. Apparently, he's now tryin' to prove-up on a place called Blackbone Flag. Sound like anyone we know?'

'So that's why you're here.' Will eyed Emer keenly. 'It's my land you want.'

Emer responded with a laugh and a shake of her head. 'If I'd wanted *that* I'd have stayed with the new-lifers. They've got thousands of acres set aside a bit further north. Preacher an' his wife already told me what was theirs was mine.'

Will shrugged. 'Well, all I got's one full section,' he said. 'But you help me to prove-up, make all the obligatory improvements before deadline, an' I'll extend the same sentiment. That, an' a promise.'

'There's an offer hard to refuse. Especially the *promise* bit,' Emer grinned. 'An' as luck would have it, I'm an expert on all sorts o' gates an' fences,' she added good humouredly.

25

At the same time as Will was digging foundations, Emer was trimming branches from the felled trees. Five days later, they had the sills set and had laid the lower rows of logs for the cabin. Then Will drove in the wedges to split more logs in two, and using saplings as rollers, the pair of them worked the wall logs up skids and into position.

Breathless, they sat with their backs against what would eventually be an outer wall of their home. Their faces were smeared with dirt and sweat, their clothes were torn and dirty. Although every bone in their bodies ached, they were satisfied and in high spirits.

Will was sipping fresh creek water from a tin mug when the sound of a rifle cracked out from the trees at the edge of the clearing. The bullet smashed into a corner log, barely six inches from his right shoulder. He dropped the mug and cursed, threw himself towards his gunbelt that was looped across the end of his sawbuck. But the rifle fractured the peace once more, and dirt spurted in front of his outstretched hand. He got to his feet, stood very still as a rider walked his trail-dusted mount from the deep shade of the cedars.

'Got to make us a bigger clearin',' he muttered, looked bewildered as he recognized his one-time partner, Joe Striker.

'Joe,' he called out. 'I heard you were in Yuma.'

'They wanted me to be,' Joe snarled back. 'Now, don't go gettin' any smart ideas, an' tell Emer to stay put. My argument's with you.'

'What argument? What the hell you doin' firin' at me?' Will asked holding the palms of his hands out. 'I thought we parted friends . . . more or less.'

'Huh, we never parted anythin'. Not unless you'd already got somethin' planned.'

'I don't know what you're talkin' about, Joe. An' I don't like you pointin' that gun at me.' Will was now sounding more angry than bewildered.

Emer couldn't see Joe's eyes, but she didn't like what she saw in his stance. 'What's this about, Joe?' she called out to him.

'Sounds like he ain't told you yet,' Joe replied, flicking his gaze between her and Will. 'Your man sold me out to the Arizona Rangers.'

'Like hell I did,' Will snapped back.

Joe continued as if Will hadn't said anything. 'Yeah, I found a bunch of 'em waitin' for me when I crossed the Gila. They knew where I was comin' *from* an' where I was likely headin' *to*. Ranger told me they'd done a deal with someone.'

'I ain't spoken to any goddamn rangers,' Will shouted back. 'I ain't spoke to *anyone* about you. Why the hell should I?'

Joe's mouth twisted with frustration. 'Money?' he suggested bitingly. 'Maybe to give you a free run with Emer? You didn't want me turnin' up to spoil your courtin'.'

For the moment, Will's anger turned to derision. 'You're bearin' a mighty high opinion o' yourself, ain't you, Joe?' he said.

'Yeah, it's an absurd accusation,' Emer put in hotly. 'You were never in the runnin', Joe. You weren't ever on the same track.'

'But *he* thought I was,' Joe insisted.

'Oh no he didn't,' Will snapped back. Then he cursed again, shook his head at the futility 'You better believe it, Joe. The three of us agreed on a three-way split. All I did was cover Emer's tracks as best I could. I struck north, never had the time or the inclination to sell you out.'

'It had to be you. Who else? Who else would've known where we were?'

'For Chris'sakes, Joe, there's been a whole bunch who could've taken a guess at that. Those who want you an' me *both*. An' don't forget, one or two o' them rangers could track a bee through a blue norther.' Thinking he was nearing some sort of truce, a moment for consideration, Will took a step forward.

But Joe adjusted his sighting. 'Stop right there, Will,' he warned. 'I ain't goin' to face you down. You know I can't pull a Colt like I used to, but I'll give you time to make a play. I can see your Colt,' he said, as he levered another shell up into the breech of his rifle.

'Joe, this is crazy,' Emer's voice rang out across the clearing. Her voice was near to breaking now and her features were taut with anguish.

Will didn't waste his breath with any protest, was no longer in the frame of mind for persuasion. He could hear and see that Joe was determined to go through with some sort of gunfight. Nothing would stop him now — he'd gone through too much suffering for too long for that — and he wasn't the backing-down type.

But there was something at the back of Will's mind that made him question whether Joe would really shoot him dead. It was after he'd ducked, made the desperate dive for his Colt, that he decided Joe wouldn't — even above the crash of the next rifle shot.

He hit the ground and went into a forward roll, came up against the sawbuck where he'd looped his gun rig. Straight off he wondered why he hadn't been hit. With a levelled rifle, Joe couldn't have missed him at that range. Yeah, that's it, he thought. Joe was more anger than action, after all. Then he heard Emer scream his name.

He reached for his Colt, spun around as he raised it. But Joe was hatless now, collapsing, falling from the saddle with blood pouring down his face. Will watched helpless as Joe crashed to the ground and lay still. Then he looked out to the ridge and his heart sank when he saw the half-dozen horsemen pounding down the slope with their guns blazing.

'Get behind the wall,' he yelled at

Emer, and she ran and dived head first over the low run of wall logs. With bullets raking the timbers and hewn stumps in front of him, he snapped two fast shots at the riders as they closed in. Then he rammed the Colt into his waist band, dropped into a crouch before making a run and a leap for his rifle. His body jerked as lead burned across his left shoulder, cursed when he felt warm blood run down his arm.

He got a hand to his rifle, turned on to his stomach and levered up a shell. Emer had dragged Joe's rifle behind cover of the logs, was shooting with gritty concentration One of the riders fell from his saddle and, as the others immediately spread, Will recognized Lester Kewell and his henchman, Newton Brass, who'd obviously recovered some from being shot on the day of the ballot. Then, as they rode closer, he cursed vehemently when he saw that Ralph Finn was riding with them. He assumed the other three riders were Kewell's payroll ranch-hands.

'Thanks for that, Joe,' he shouted to no one in particular, realizing that Joe's appearance had simply been the eye of the storm.

26

Clearly not reckoning on much resistance, the riders came in shooting, intent on razing anything that moved.

For the shortest moment, Will grinned at Emer's prowess. Her bullet hit Newton Brass, took him clear of the saddle. Another rider's horse shied in terror before veering away. Will put a bullet somewhere in the top of his leg and the man slumped forward with his arms clinging to the mount's neck. The man who was riding alongside him, took one dispirited look, then fled for the safety of the cedar stands.

'That's what you get when you mix with a fairground shootist,' Will yelled out.

Lester Kewell's face was greasy-grey as he raced his horse for cover. 'Goddamn you to hell, Ralph. I told you to nail Johnson,' he bellowed at Finn.

The saloon owner attempted to jump his horse over a pile of trimmed branches, but it landed awkwardly and went down, kneeling on a foreleg. Kewell swung himself away from the saddle, ran a few steps towards where Emer raised herself to see how badly he'd been hit.

It was a mistake, and Kewell reached out and grabbed her viciously, wrenched the rifle from her grasp and dragged her up and over the wall. He threw an arm around her and pulled her in tight, used her as a shield as he pulled his Colt for striking back at Will.

Kewell's hurried shot missed, but the man wasn't Will's only problem: Ralph Finn was on top of him now. He tried to dodge, but Finn's boot caught him a blow on the side of the head and sent him spinning. He dropped his rifle, went head-over-heels as Finn wheeled to level his Colt. The man got off two fast shots, but Will had drawn his own six-gun, twisted around and fired before he went down.

Will's bullet struck Finn square in the chest. Mule town's sheriff grunted fatally, waved his Colt in a futile gesture as another bullet hit him. Then he fell sideways, and hit the ground very hard.

'That's for you an' your snaky kin,' Will rasped. 'Joe Striker would probably have done it, if you hadn't have busted his fingers.'

Frantically, Kewell was looking from side to side, startled to see he was now alone. Emer took advantage of his panic; with renewed spirit, she set her neck muscles and sank her teeth cruelly into the flesh of his gun arm. Kewell let out a rasping scream, dragged his hand free and smashed her across the face.

The blow knocked Emer away, and Kewell, now frantic and vulnerable, spun to bring up his gun. But he was too late. With only one bullet remaining in the cylinder of his Colt, Will had made a steady aim. Kewell took the bullet in his heart, was lifeless before his face smacked into the pummelled grass.

The air reeked of acrid gunsmoke, and thin vaporous ribbons curled across the clearing. Emer was sitting stunned, holding her fingertips to her mouth, the side of her face.

'It was my last bullet. He gave me no choice,' Will said, running towards her.

'I thought you wanted me to help with improvements to your land, not the disposition o' your neighbours,' she said quietly.

Will shrugged. 'I know, I lied,' he said with a tired, wry grin. 'I remembered you sayin' you'd always been a crack shot.' He knelt beside her and she pulled a face when she saw the blood oozing from the wound in his shoulder.

'It's nothin',' he said, turning at the movement he caught out of the corner of his eye. It was Ralph Finn, and using one elbow and one hand, he was dragging himself towards his gun.

Will strode across and kicked it out of his reach, looked down at the man who had blood bubbling from a corner of his mouth.

'You chose badly for the end game, Finn,' he rasped. 'Kewell didn't have the guts for this kind o' work. He hired others. Huh, even *they* turned tail.'

Finn moved his head. 'Yeah, odds ain't good when you're tryin' to get even. Old Lloyd told me as much.'

'He should know. I hear he ain't ever stormin' any puncheons again.'

'Yeah, ain't he the lucky one.' With that, Muletown's errant sheriff gave a muffled cough; he was dead within two minutes.

The bullet that had brought Joe down, had ploughed a deep furrow along the side of his scalp, above his left ear. There was a lot of blood running across his face and he was still unconscious.

Will and Emer looked down at him with concern.

'Well, he's still with us. Maybe the rest'll do him good.' Will looked on as Emer trickled water across the stricken man's forehead.

'He ain't dead then?' a voice from behind them, asked.

They spun, but Will didn't lift the Colt as he saw the shield on the stranger's shirt. In any case Leo Tuckwell was covering him with a big, double-action Colt.

'Where the hell did you come from?' Will asked, returning the ranger's level gaze.

'Flagstaff originally. Phoenix more recent,' Tuckwell replied coolly. 'But right here's where I've been for the last hour, just watchin.'

Will gestured towards Finn. 'He used to be the sheriff o' some Godforsaken hole called Muletown. He's also the one who shot this feller. His name's Striker an' he's a partner o' mine.'

'Yeah, I know. An' you're the one they call Will Johnson. The girl's Emer Sparrow, an' it looks like the pair o' you got a yen to settle down,' he asserted.

Will nodded slowly as the ranger looked around.

'That's right, me an' my wife.' Will paused then grinned. 'In the eyes o' some folk we're already married.'

Emer shook her head good naturedly. 'But I'll never say, 'I do' until he gets rid o' them whiskers,' she said, with a careful, measured look at Tuckwell.

The ranger responded with a perceptive glance back. 'Personally, unless there was good need, I'd never trust a man with a beard. I'd always think he was hidin' somethin',' he said tellingly.

'I ain't hidin' the fact that the odds were stacked against us. But now we can do some real work an' still prove-up on time,' Will said, hardly daring to hope that maybe Tuckwell was offering them some kind of a chance.

'Given a fair wind, I think we'll make good homesteaders,' Emer said, offering a tentative smile.

'Well, there ain't anybody much left alive to cause you any more trouble,' Tuckwell answered. 'But I guess I'll know where to find you if needs be.' He glanced down at Joe. 'I suppose gettin' near to havin' your brains blown out's better than five years breakin' rocks.'

'You could tell me somethin' before you haul out o' here,' Will said. 'Who was it told you where to look for Joe Striker?'

'Ha. Someone he should probably have killed in a place called Slater Wells. The sheriff there put out a hundred-dollar reward for his hide. With that sort o' money on offer, it could've been anyone between here an' there.'

'Yeah,' Will said understandingly. 'An' thanks for goin' back to Arizona empty-handed. You rode a long way.'

'Keeps me away from a lot o' temptation, an' I get paid either way,' Tuckwell explained. 'I'll get someone from Indian Hat to send out a garbage wagon. No need for you to dig all these good folk into your land. Tell me, would you be the kind o' workin' girl who carries a tune?' he asked Emer as a parting thought.

'No. *She* went off with a party o' blessed emigrants. *I've* got a voice like one o' them Gulf Toads,' Emer replied with a poker face.

'Yeah, I bet,' the ranger said, and nodded contentedly. Then he lifted a final leave-taking hand and walked away, back to the ridge where he'd hitched his mount.

A moment later, Will turned on his heel and walked over to Joe. He looked down into the man's pain-racked face and knelt beside him.

'When you get better, I suggest you don't go ridin' anywhere near Slater Wells,' he advised.

'I was thinkin' you could stay *here* awhile,' Emer offered. 'Maybe help us build up the place.'

'Thanks. I'm usually associated with takin' places apart. I guess things have changed,' Joe said.

THE END

We do hope that you have enjoyed reading this large print book.

Did you know that all of our titles are available for purchase?

We publish a wide range of high quality large print books including:
Romances, Mysteries, Classics
General Fiction
Non Fiction and Westerns

Special interest titles available in large print are:
The Little Oxford Dictionary
Music Book, Song Book
Hymn Book, Service Book

Also available from us courtesy of Oxford University Press:
Young Readers' Dictionary
(large print edition)
Young Readers' Thesaurus
(large print edition)

For further information or a free brochure, please contact us at:
Ulverscroft Large Print Books Ltd.,
The Green, Bradgate Road, Anstey,
Leicester, LE7 7FU, England.
Tel: (00 44) 0116 236 4325
Fax: (00 44) 0116 234 0205

BLIND JUSTICE AT WEDLOCK

Ross Morton

When Clint Brennan finds two men kidnapping his wife Belle, he's shot and left for dead. However, though he's been blinded, he realises his wife has gone. So, not giving way, Clint sets out after his wife's abductors, with his dog and astride his donkey. Belle, meanwhile, believes he's dead and when she's rescued by a rich man, she's told it's time to start again . . . All this violence, betrayal and lies will end at Wedlock, amidst flames and bullets.

COLORADO CLEAN-UP

Corba Sunman

Provost Captain Slade Moran arrives from Fort Benson, Colorado, to investigate the disappearance of an army payroll and its military secret. A grim trail has taken him to the empty payroll coach and its murdered escort, with one soldier mysteriously missing. Moran is led to Moundville where he's confronted by desperate men plotting to steal a gold mine. Embroiled in double-cross and mayhem, Moran fears he will fail in his duty. Against all odds, can he succeed?

CANNON FOR HIRE

Doug Thorne

In the autumn of 1897, men flock to the wild Yukon Territory, searching for gold. But Tom Cannon, a one-time cavalry officer, has a different reason for making the hazardous trek north. Hired to find Emmet Lawrence — a greenhorn who'd disappeared seeking his fortune — Cannon searches the icy wastes and snow-capped mountains and draws a blank. No one remembers Lawrence, or knows his whereabouts. Then something happens that Cannon hasn't allowed for — Emmet Lawrence comes looking for him . . .